PUFFIN BOOKS

Editor: Kaye Webb

CATWEAZLE

Catweazle was a magician who lived in the eleventh century, but however hard he tried, his spells hardly ever worked.

Then one day was different. First of all he had two bad omens – a bad dream and an owl hooting in daylight. Then Norman soldiers tried to capture him, so in desperation he used some magic, and it worked! The only trouble was that it had worked in the wrong way: Catweazle flew through Time instead of Space, and ended up in a place called Hexwood Farm, nine centuries later, where of course he thought everything he saw – motor cars, telephones, electric light ('Electrickery') – all happened by magic.

How Catweazle is befriended by the farmer's son, Carrot, and how he finds his feet in the twentieth century, while hiding from the world in a water tower, makes a riotously funny story, as anyone who has watched the London Week-end Television serial of *Catweazle* will know. We are delighted to have George Adamson's illustrations to go with it, and to tell you that all the spells are taken from the collections of real witches.

For readers of eight and over.

RICHARD CARPENTER

Illustrated by George Adamson

'The art is true
but there be but a few that
have skill in it.'

*The Anatomy of
Melancholy*

PENGUIN BOOKS

Penguin Books Ltd, Harmondsworth, Middlesex, England
Penguin Books Inc., 7110 Ambassador Road, Baltimore, Maryland 21207, U.S.A.
Penguin Books Australia Ltd, Ringwood, Victoria, Australia

—

First published in Puffin Books 1970

—

Copyright © Richard Carpenter, 1970
Copyright © London Weekend International Limited, 1970

—

Made and printed in Great Britain
by Cox & Wyman Ltd,
London, Reading and Fakenham
Set in Linotype Georgian

TO ANNIE

For all her 'electrickery'

CONTENTS

ACKNOWLEDGEMENTS

THIS book grew out of a television series and therefore my thanks are due to everyone who worked on it. In particular I would like to thank Joy Whitby, its instigator and my continual help. Without her, Catweazle would probably never have happened.

My thanks are also due to Quentin Lawrence for all the warmth and fun he added when directing the series, and finally to Teresa Wills who helped me so much with the actual book.

1

THE FLIGHT

IT was still dark in the cave. Outside in the forest, the birds screamed and chattered. Catweazle, who had been dreaming of monsters, woke with a sudden cry and shivered with relief. He scratched himself, sneezed, removed a moth from his beard, and sat up. Such a dream was a bad omen, he thought uneasily as he rubbed his thin chest, and climbed stiffly from the pile of hay he slept in.

The Sacred Fire was almost out, so he knelt down, his joints cracking, and blew on the embers. Wood ash rose in the air and settled on his beard, but the fire glowed red, and he soon had it warming him again.

The firelight flickered over the walls of the cave which were covered with magical designs. There were pentacles, spirals and rings within rings. Most of them had been used for various spells, but some had just been doodles to use up the paint, especially the spirals.

Holding his hands out to the fire, Catweazle thought again of his dream. 'An omen – ay, an omen. Mayhap of doom,' he muttered.

A rather fat toad crawled out of the shadows. It was Touchwood, Catweazle's familiar. All magicians had familiars; they were more than just pets, they helped with the magic. Touchwood didn't help much but Catweazle was fond of him, and it gave him someone to boss around.

Touchwood croaked as he crawled towards the fire. He didn't like it. It had once shot a spark at him, hitting him on the leg, and Touchwood had disappeared under a stone for nearly a week. He stared balefully at Catweazle.

The magician and his familiar weren't at their best, first thing in the morning.

'I dreamed of monsters, Touchwood,' said Catweazle, turning the pages of a huge book. ' 'Tis an omen of doom.'

Touchwood crawled carefully round the fire, keeping well clear of it. He wasn't interested in omens of doom, he was looking for spiders.

Catweazle continued to search the tattered pages. The book was his Grimoire, a collection of magical writings. The pages were all different sizes and thicknesses, which made them difficult to turn. Some were of parchment, others were of vellum, and some were thin sheets of leather. It was the strangest book in the world.

It was full of spells for every situation: healing spells and harming spells, making and breaking spells, spells to make things grow, and spells to make sure that nothing would grow. There were spells so secret that even Catweazle didn't know what they were for, curses and incantations, conjurations and Words of Power – everything, in fact, to do with Demons, Devils, Dragons, Spirits, and Monsters. It was all written in the curling, wriggling, cabalistic alphabet, part script, part heiroglyph. Some of it went across the pages, and some went up and down. Some even went diagonally from corner to corner. Little drawings of birds, butterflies and fish, shells and tiny flowers, covered the margins.

Catweazle stopped turning the pages; he had found what he had been looking for. ' "If thou wouldst protect thyself from the evil shadows of the night",' he read, ' "make thou a circle, and with thy knife, point to the four winds, saying the while, Sator, Arepo, Tenet, Opera, Rotas." '

He nodded approvingly. This was one of his favourite incantations. After all, it was the same forwards or backwards, and if a square was made of the words, it could be read up and down as well.

```
S A T O R
A R E P O
T E N E T
O P E R A
R O T A S
```

Catweazle was sure that this talisman would protect him, and, carrying the book, he went over to his magic circle, a ring of sand surrounding a rather badly drawn star. At each of the five points of the star was a candle. He had made them himself and they didn't burn very well. They weren't particularly black either, as the book had specified, but he had said all the right words while he made them, and the words were the important thing.

He lit the candles, after nearly burning his fingers, and then, standing in the middle of the circle, he drew his ceremonial knife from the sheath he wore round his scrawny neck. The magic name Adamcos was engraved down the blade. Catweazle was very proud of his dagger. He had made it himself, carefully following the instructions in the book, and as well as being very magical it cut rather well.

Waving it to the North, to the East, to the South, and, finally, to the West, he intoned the Words of Power. Then, sheathing the knife, he stepped carefully out of the circle with his fingers crossed.

Touchwood was stolidly chewing an earwig. This made Catweazle remember how hungry he was. His belly rumbled; he was very empty. He thought of delicacies like roots and berries and his belly rumbled again. Blowing out the candles and putting some more branches on the Sacred Fire, he climbed the rough steps and crawled out of the cave.

The sky was turning pink above the trees as he pushed aside the bushes that concealed the entrance, and, straightening up, sniffed all the interesting smells of the early morning. It was going to be another hot day.

Catweazle was very dirty. His hair was wild and matted but his eyes were bright and his wrinkled brown face emphasized their blueness. He looked around, sneezed, coughed, scratched himself, and set off through the forest.

For an old man, he moved surprisingly quickly. He seemed almost to hop along, and he turned his head from side to side like a chicken, as he searched for food. His sharp eyes missed nothing. A wild boar snuffled against a fallen tree, ripping the bark away with its curved tusks, and took no notice of the thin ragged figure running past.

Catweazle's dream was still bothering him, and, occasionally, he glanced behind him, just in case there was a monster following, and muttered a few quick spells to give himself a bit more protection. Then he stopped suddenly, seeing his breakfast ahead.

At the other side of a forest pool there was a tree and from it grew a large pink fungus with white spots. Catweazle's mouth watered. He knew it was safe to eat because the birds were pecking at it.

He skirted the pool as carefully as Touchwood had gone round the Sacred Fire. Catweazle was terrified of water and kept well away from it. He had once cast his horoscope and had learnt that water might mean a special danger, and that he would be wise to avoid it.

He reached the tree, and he broke off a piece of the fungus, and bit into it, holding it like a bun. It was delicious, and very filling. He sat down, munching contentedly, and watched the deer coming down to the pool to drink. He would try the Flying Spell again today, he thought.

He had worked for years at the Flying Spell, but, so far, he had never left the ground. He couldn't understand it. He said all the right Words of Power and made all the potions properly, but nothing worked. There must be something he always forgot, but what was it? He twisted his scraggy beard round one dirty finger. And then it happened.

An owl appeared on a low branch nearby – and hooted.

Catweazle leapt to his feet, his bony knees knocking together under his robe and his white hair standing on end. Quickly he raised his left hand, 'Gab, gaba, agaba,' he gasped, and blew on his magic yellow thumb-ring. Owls that hooted in the daylight were very bad luck.

The charm had no effect on the owl. It merely blinked, swivelled its head round and gave another hoot. 'B-b-b-bird of Night, hoot not,' stammered Catweazle, trying hard to remember the owl spell. 'Er . . . Feathered Omen, hoot not,' he continued uneasily, 'Son of Tanit, hoot not!'

The owl stared at him for a moment, hooted again, and then flew off over his head. Catweazle ducked, almost falling over backwards. He was very frightened. First monsters, and now birds of ill omen. He turned in the direction of his cave and scampered home.

When he reached the cave, he almost fell down the steps in his eagerness to hide. 'Oh Touchwood, Touchwood,' he gasped, collapsing on the floor, 'the Bird of Night doth hoot by day. Ill luck, ill luck!'

Touchwood, who was squatting on the book of magic, remained calm, almost impassive. His tongue flicked out at a passing fly, and the fly vanished. He gulped, croaked reassuringly at his master, and crawled off the book.

Gradually Catweazle's panic subsided and he picked up the book. Powerful magic had to be made – and quickly.

After studying the book for several minutes, he began to assemble a weird collection of plants and herbs on the floor in front of him. Hemlock and foxglove, ivy and deadnettle, henbane and marigold: putting all the bits of the various plants into a stone bowl, he began to grind them to pulp with a long piece of flint. As he did so, he recited spells from the book, using Touchwood to hold down the pages like a four-legged paper-weight, but Touchwood kept wandering off in search of spiders and the pages would turn so that Catweazle read the wrong spells.

'I will feed thee anon, Grizzle-guts,' he muttered, replacing the toad on the book, and he pounded away at the mess in the bowl and began to howl out a long incantation at the top of his voice.

He was so absorbed in protecting himself that he didn't notice the group of figures peering down at him from the mouth of the cave. It was a party of Norman soldiers, who stared with astonishment as Catweazle began skipping round his magic circle, sprinkling the crushed plants on the ground.

'Salmay, Dalmay, Adonay!' yelled Catweazle, flinging bits of plant all over the place.

The Normans were bewildered. They drew their swords, and, reversing them, held the hilts like crosses in front of their faces. They weren't taking any chances.

'Guard me, O Spirits!' sang Catweazle.

The Normans gripped their swords. What strange magic was the English sorcerer making? 'I conjure thee,' continued Catweazle, his voice echoing round the cave. The Normans prepared to attack. 'Tetragrammaton!' shouted Catweazle at the top of his voice. The Normans charged down the steps into the cave and Catweazle turned in sudden terror as he saw the armed men thundering towards him. As two of them grabbed at him, he ducked under their reaching hands and they overbalanced and fell into each other's arms. A third soldier thrust at him with his sword but Catweazle hurled his magic book straight at him and the man fell over backwards to avoid it. A fourth, however, caught Catweazle offguard, and gripped his shoulder, but like lightning Catweazle sank his teeth in the soldier's unprotected hand, and the burly Norman let go with a yell. The cave seemed full of lumbering figures crashing against each other. Then Catweazle stamped out the Sacred Fire and plunged the cave into darkness.

The advantage was all his now. He could see as clearly in the dark as he could by daylight, and he wove his way between all the flailing arms and legs, picked up Touchwood, and stumbled up the steps.

As he ran off into the forest, putting Touchwood into his special pocket, Catweazle looked back. The Normans were beginning to stagger out through the bushes, waving their swords and blinking in the sunlight.

'Fools!' shouted Catweazle, 'Norman fools! I will lead thee a dance,' and he thumbed his nose at them. The sight of the bony old man hopping about between the trees and jeering at them infuriated the soldiers, and they gave chase. Catweazle stuck out his tongue and then scampered off into the forest.

He hated the Normans. Only a few years earlier, he had watched a great battle from the southern edge of the forest near the tiny village of Hastings. He had seen the shield wall broken by the charging horsemen and watched the pitiless rain of arrows, and when the English army was routed and the forest full of running men, Catweazle had gone back to his cave to tell Touchwood that the end of the world was at hand.

He'd show them, he thought to himself, as he led the infuriated Normans deeper and deeper into the forest. He led them through brambles and stinging nettles where they would never catch him. Leaving them searching in some bushes, he climbed a tree and rested, while below him the confused and cursing men slashed away at the undergrowth with their swords. Then, bewildered by Catweazle's sudden vanishing trick, they began to move away.

Catweazle started to climb down the far side of the tree, but, just as he reached the lowest branch and prepared to jump down, Touchwood did an unforgivable thing: he put his head out of the pocket, and croaked loudly. The Normans turned, Catweazle lost his balance and fell out of the tree, and the chase was on again.

Catweazle was spitting with fury at Touchwood's stupidity, and he ran as fast as he could towards a stretch of swampy ground. There was a secret path across it that he knew well and he ran on to it without hesitating. The Normans followed, and one by one they slipped off the path and began to sink into the mud. They wallowed about, swearing at Catweazle and trying vainly to find the path again. At the other side of the swamp, he turned and mocked them.

'Know that I am Catweazle,' he called. 'Thou canst not catch me, thou wood-lice!' And he left them struggling in the mud.

He chuckled gleefully to himself as he made his way across a clearing, but there were three more soldiers crouching in the bushes and as he drew level with them they leapt out on him. Try as they might they could not hold him. He wriggled out of their grasp, tripped one of them and, breaking away, headed down an overgrown track, his brown robe flapping round him. Too late he realized he was heading straight for a lake and that he was trapped.

As he ran out of the trees at the water's edge, he looked wildly round, but there was no escape. The Normans fanned out behind him and advanced slowly with their swords at the ready.

Catweazle dithered, not knowing what to do. He wished he hadn't fooled with them. They were angry

now and might beat him or, what was worse, lock him up. He looked at the lake and shuddered.

A tall pine had fallen with its topmost branches nearly a hundred feet out in the water. As the Normans closed in, Catweazle scrambled on the fallen tree and, balancing precariously, walked out over the lake.

He stood on the tree and looked back at the Normans watching him from the bank. A swallow darted over the lake, almost touching the water. If only he could fly, he thought desperately.

'Let me fly, O Spirits! Bear me hence,' he implored flapping his arms wildly, as he saw one of the Normans beginning to climb on to the fallen tree.

'Nothing works,' moaned Catweazle, and then, putting everything into a final plea, he called for his magic to help him.

'Sunandum! Hurandos! Let me fly! Salmay! Dalmay! Adonay!' and, still flapping his arms, Catweazle jumped into the air, and with a tremendous splash, fell into the lake.

2

HEXWOOD FARM

CATWEAZLE spluttered to the surface. His bedraggled hair, streaming with water, was crowned with a piece of slimy weed. Standing up and blinking the drops from his eyes, he was very surprised to find that the water only came up to his waist.

He was standing in a small pond. The lake had vanished. So had the Normans. A duck swam round him quacking angrily, while, nearby, several cows looked at him with mild surprise. One of them mooed at him.

He had flown! That was it, he had flown!

He waded out of the pond, anxious to leave the water behind him. The duck stuck its tail in the air and dived for food as Catweazle felt in his dripping robe for Touchwood, but the pocket was empty.

'Touchwood, where art thou?' called Catweazle, but there was no answer. The toad had vanished.

Catweazle was very upset. Perhaps Touchwood had fallen out while they had been flying. It was an awful thought, and Catweazle tried to console himself by imagining Touchwood falling into a tree, perhaps even a bird's nest.

A dog barked in the distance, making Catweazle jump. He wondered how far he had flown and if there were Normans near. He looked around for somewhere to hide. At the other side of the field was an old barn, and still dripping with water, he stumbled across to it.

He peered in, sniffing suspiciously, and reassured that the barn was empty, crept inside. It was large and smelt of straw, a warm, comforting smell. Catweazle stood carefully looking in every corner while a puddle formed at his feet, and a faint rumbling began somewhere outside the barn. It was like no sound he had ever heard before and as it approached it became louder and louder, until it was a great roaring, shaking the earth. It was coming nearer, it was coming into the barn! The noise was deafening, as Catweazle, blowing frantically on his magic thumb-ring, backed in horror from the barn doors.

It was the monster from his dream! Its great red head poked its way into the barn. With a cry, Catweazle dived behind a pile of straw bales and buried his face in his hands.

A large tractor with a front loader attached to it drove into the barn and came to a stop. Sam Woodyard, a big, raw-boned farm-worker, switched off the engine and turned to the boy sitting beside him.

'Von Trips, his name was. Great driver he was an' all. Drove for Ferrari mostly. They don't make racing drivers like him any more.'

Edward Bennet, nicknamed Carrot because of his red hair, jumped down from the tractor and began to unload turkey boxes.

'What time's the programme?'

'Half nine. Should be a good 'un.'

'Your telly's working again then?' asked Carrot, dumping the boxes near Catweazle's hiding-place.

'Yes, but I'm comin' back here to watch it – yer Dad said I could. Mum always watches "Memory Lane" you see, and that's on the other channel.'

Catweazle peered through a gap in the bales. Who were these strange sorcerers, he wondered. He eyed their magic chariot with fear and tried to understand the gibberish they were talking.

Sam went over to an old bike leaning against the wall.

' "They Diced with Death", it's called. Ought to be full

of spins. One mile an hour too fast is enough you know. Even the best of 'em do it,' and he put on his cycle clips.

'Sounds dangerous,' said Carrot.

'No, not really. The cars are so low slung you see. You'd never turn one of 'em over. Mind you, if there's one close behind, it could be dangerous!' Sam leant over the bike. 'I'll never forget Mike Hawthorne at Silverstone. Spun off, he did, in front of the stands and then spun on again – and he still kept the lead.'

'Fantastic,' said Carrot.

'Soon as I git Apollo Twelve goin' agin I'll show yer how he did it.'

Apollo Twelve, Sam's car, was hardly ever on the road, and it was only by spending hours underneath it that he ever got it going at all.

'I'll get a gear-box from somewhere,' he said, mounting his bike. 'Now don't forgit. Nine thirty, "They Diced with Death". See ya, Carrot,' and he rode out of the barn.

Catweazle, who had found this conversation beyond him, watched with amazement as the man balanced himself on two wheels and silently rode out through the door. Truly, they were sorcerers! He shivered and then, as the boy once more came near carrying the boxes with the magic signs on them, he sneezed loudly.

Carrot stopped piling the boxes. Catweazle sneezed again, and the boy crossed to the magician's hiding-place. Pulling away one of the bales he stared at the dripping figure.

'Who the heck are you?' gasped Carrot.

Catweazle's teeth chattered and drops of water fell from his beard.

'Come out,' said Carrot, thinking Catweazle was a tramp.

Catweazle remained where he was.

'Look, you've got to come out.'

'Art thou Norman?' managed Catweazle after a moment or two.

'No. My name's Edward,' Carrot replied, still very taken aback.

'What is this place?' asked the magician fearfully.

'Hexwood Turkey Farm. This is private property, and you're trespassing.' Carrot was as pleasant as he could be about it, but he knew that if his father found a tramp in the barn he would be furious.

Catweazle pointed at the tractor. 'I fear it,' he said, trembling.

'What, Lulu?' Carrot laughed. 'You're not scared of a tractor, are you?'

'It roars like the damned.'

'Noise can't hurt you,' said Carrot. 'Now come on out!'

Slowly, Catweazle came out of his hiding-place. He stared at the tractor and blew on his magician's ring.

'Roar not, O magic chariot,' he said.

Carrot looked at the old tramp. He was obviously a little mad. Then he noticed the puddles underneath Catweazle's feet.

'You're soaking wet,' he said, but Catweazle was too absorbed in the magic chariot to hear him. 'Canst thou command it?' he asked. 'Hast *thou* the Power?'

Carrot climbed up into the driving seat. 'Look, it's only a tractor,' he said, and switched on the engine. With a cry of fear, Catweazle scrambled into an empty barrel and disappeared. Carrot was still laughing and revving the engine, when his father, the owner of the farm, came into the barn.

'How many times have I told you not to play with the tractor,' said Mr Bennet angrily. 'Switch it off.' He was in a bad mood. The wrong turkey feed had been delivered from Hoopers and it meant further delays. Carrot climbed down, casting a glance at the barrel.

'Just leave it alone, otherwise no trip to London, d'you understand?' Carrot looked at his father's angry face. 'Yes, Dad,' he said quietly, handing him the keys.

'Sam's gone, has he?' said Mr Bennet, looking round. Winston, his dog, was sniffing round the barrel. 'There's a rat in there,' he continued, and grasped his stick.

Carrot ran past him to get to the barrel first, and peered down at the cowering Catweazle. 'No rats, Dad,' he said.

'What's that terrible pong, then?' said Mr Bennet, sniffing.

'What pong, Dad?' asked Carrot innocently. It was Catweazle of course.

'Can't you smell it?' said Mr Bennet, screwing up his nose. 'We'd better have a good clean out tomorrow. Next thing's to move the birds from No. Two shed,' and Mr Bennet left the barn.

Catweazle poked his head out of the barrel and looked at Carrot.

'I starve, boy,' he said, and his belly rumbled loudly.

Carrot didn't know what to do. He had got into trouble the previous week for feeding a tramp, and when four of them had turned up the next day, Mr Bennet had told him that they were trying to run a farm not a soup kitchen and that Carrot wasn't to give food to anyone. Catweazle certainly looked very hungry, though, and eventually Carrot said, 'All right, but you mustn't come to the house. You stay here, and I'll bring you something.'

Catweazle nodded. He would take the food, find his way back to the forest, wait for night and then go back to his cave. He ducked down again as Mr Bennet came back. 'Come on, Carrot,' he said.

'Coming Dad,' Carrot called after his father. 'Don't go out of here!' he hissed at the barrel as he went to the door.

Catweazle surfaced again. 'Is this place known to the Normans?' he asked anxiously.

'The Normans?' said Carrot.

'Ay, boy, the Norman invaders.'

'What are you talking about? The Normans were hundreds of years ago.'

Catweazle looked at the boy. What did he mean? He began to feel something was very wrong.

'Hundreds of years?' his voice quavered.

'Yes, of course. Round about nine hundred,' said the boy, and ran out of the barn after his father.

For a long time Catweazle stood transfixed, staring at the barn doors, then slowly he clutched his head.

'Nine hundred years,' he whispered to himself, and holding his fingers in front of his face, he slowly counted to nine.

'Nine hundred years since the Normans?' he muttered. 'Nine hundred years since this morning?' Then he had flown indeed!

Hexwood farmhouse was old, square, and rather dilapidated. The Bennets never had either time or money to restore it and since the death of his wife the previous year, Mr Bennet had struggled through one crisis after another; sinovitis had killed off large numbers of turkeys, and the bank was refusing to lend him any more money. He did his best, but he found it difficult to give much time to Carrot, preoccupied as he was with the farm.

'I'm going up to the pub for a game of darts,' he told Carrot later that evening as the two of them cleared the supper things from the kitchen table. Carrot was secretly pleased. It meant he would have no difficulty taking the food to the old tramp in the barn.

'No sawing on the kitchen table, right?' said his father, putting on his jacket and preparing to leave. 'I'd like to come back to a reasonably tidy place for once.'

'Right, Dad,' Carrot grinned. He waited until he heard the sound of the truck going up the lane and then he went through into the scullery and began to make some sandwiches. He made good chunky ones, with thick slices of cheese, took some cold turkey from the fridge and some apples from the fruit bowl, and put the whole lot in a carrier bag. He was just about to leave for the barn when there was a knock on the door. It was Sam.

'Starts in five minutes,' said Sam, coming in and shutting the door behind him.

'What does?' said Carrot.

' "They Diced with Death"! Haven't forgotten have yer?'

'Er ... no. Of course not,' replied Carrot, putting the bag behind a chair and taking Sam through the hall to the sitting-room.

'I'll be back in a minute,' he said, switching on the television. 'Shan't be long.' Carrot ran back to the kitchen, and slipped quietly out of the scullery door with the bag of food.

The farmyard was dark and he tiptoed across it so that the turkeys wouldn't set up their gobbling and flapping. Creeping into the barn, he called softly.

'Are you still here?'

The old man's voice came out of the darkness, 'Ay, boy.'

'Where?'

'Here!'

Carrot switched on the powerful working light. With a cry of terror, Catweazle reared up in the barrel, his hands warding off the sudden dazzling brightness. The barrel crashed over, spilling him on to the floor.

'Blinded! Blinded by witchcraft!' he moaned as he tried to crawl back into the barrel on all-fours.

Carrot switched off the light and groped his way over to Catweazle.

'What on earth's the matter with you?' he said, trying to pull the old man out.

'I see again,' said Catweazle with relief. 'Hast thou lifted the curse?'

'No, I've turned off the light.'

Catweazle slowly backed out of the barrel. 'What magic didst thou use?' he asked fearfully

'What d'you mean, magic?' said Carrot, finding his way back to the switch. 'It's electricity,' and he turned on the light again.

With another yell, Catweazle fell on his knees, covering his eyes, but after a moment he slowly took his hands away from his face and screwing up his eyes, blinked at the light hanging from the roof of the barn. Then, turning to Carrot, he bowed low in obeisance.

'Master!' he whispered.

'Eh?' said Carrot.

'Let me serve thee!'

'What!'

'Teach me thy elec-trickery – that I may do it.'

'Do what?' said Carrot.

'Put the sun in a bottle,' said Catweazle, pointing up at the light-bulb.

Carrot helped the old man to his feet and took him over to the switch. 'Look,' he said, putting his finger on it. 'It's electricity,' and he switched the light off and on again a few times while Catweazle stood amazed at the power of the young magician.

Back in the farmhouse, Sam was looking for Carrot. Trying to get a better picture on the television set, he had twiddled the knobs until he had lost it altogether. When he went into the kitchen he saw the barn light flashing on and off, on and off, across the dark farmyard. In the barn, Catweazle, mastering his fear, was happily playing with the light switch.

'What's Carrot playin' at?' muttered Sam, and left the house to investigate.

'All right,' said Carrot, 'that's enough. Here's your food,' and he held out the carrier bag. Catweazle was about to take it when he stopped and drew back, looking towards the door.

'My thumbs are pricking,' he said. 'Someone comes!' and, running into a dark corner, he hid behind a pile of turkey crates.

Seconds later, Sam poked his head round the door. 'What are you playin' at?' he said, as Carrot hid the carrier behind him.

'Practising Morse,' he replied. 'I thought you were watching the telly?'

'Picture's gone wrong,' said Sam rather shamefacedly, knowing it was his fault. 'Can you fix it?'

'Think so,' said Carrot.

'Well come on then. We're missin' it,' and before Carrot could do anything, Sam pushed him out of the barn in front of him.

Catweazle listened to the receding footsteps and then, drawn by the smell of the food, he sniffed his way out of the barn, and careful not to be seen, followed them across the yard.

Carrot hurriedly adjusted the television in the sitting-room and Sam once more settled down utterly absorbed as the racing cars snarled by on the screen. He didn't even notice Carrot slip out of the room behind him, and run softly back to the kitchen, where he found Catweazle, looking round in bewilderment.

'I told you to stay in the barn,' Carrot whispered putting a chair against the door as a barricade.

'I starve,' said Catweazle.

'O.K.' said Carrot, 'but you'll have to be quick,' and he retrieved the food from the scullery.

Catweazle sat down and began to wolf the sandwiches while Carrot watched him. Chewing and swallowing at the same time he stuffed the food into his mouth with both hands.

'You *are* hungry, aren't you?' said Carrot with some surprise. 'Would you like some orange juice?'

Catweazle, who had never heard of orange juice, gulped down another sandwich. 'I know not,' he mumbled through the bread and cheese.

Carrot brought him a glass. 'Try it,' he said. 'It's jolly good.'

Catweazle eyed it for a moment and then took a huge mouthful. Rising quickly, he spat it out all over the table. 'Shouldst thou seek to poison me,' he said, trembling with rage and fear, 'I will call up Demons to destroy thee!'

'You're crackers,' said Carrot, backing away.

'Nay, I am Catweazle,' the magician corrected.

'Who?'

'Catweazle,' the old man repeated. 'Hear me, young sorcerer. I come from the time when this land was conquered by William of Normandy.'

The 'young sorcerer' seemed unimpressed.

'You will tell no one?' Catweazle went on.

'No. Of course not,' said Carrot, anxious not to offend him.

'You must swear it. By Adamcos,' said Catweazle, drawing his ceremonial knife.

'Crumbs! What's that?' asked Carrot, very taken with the knife.

' 'Tis my witch knife, Adamcos. Sacred to Hecate,' explained Catweazle, puzzled that the young magician should find such elementary magic hard to understand.

He held it up in front of Carrot's face and moved it slowly from side to side.

'I swear,' intoned Catweazle.

'I swear,' repeated Carrot.

'By the Spirits of the Brazen Vessel,' the old magician continued.

'By the Spirits of the Brazen Vessel – what's that?'

'Sssh. That I will say nothing,'

'That I will say nothing,'

'Of Catweazle.'

'Of Catweazle,' finished Carrot, his eyes still following the moving knife.

' 'Tis well,' said Catweazle, sheathing Adamcos. Slowly Carrot's eyes re-focused.

'Right,' he said. 'Now don't you think you ought to push off?'

Before Catweazle had a chance to ask the boy what he meant, they were interrupted by the sound of Sam trying to get into the kitchen.

'Carrot!' he called, 'I can't get in.'

Carrot froze and pointed towards the scullery, but as Catweazle reached the door and prepared to run out into the yard, the headlights from Mr Bennet's truck swept across the windows.

'It's Dad,' hissed Carrot, grabbing Catweazle, and he pushed him once more towards the kitchen.

'What are you playin' at, Carrot?' came Sam's aggrieved voice from the hall.

'We're trapped!' whispered Carrot, bundling Catweazle over to the kitchen window as he heard the door of the truck slam and his father's approaching footsteps.

'Whither shall I go?' wailed Catweazle as Carrot frantically opened the window and tried to push him out.

'Anywhere,' he said, longing to be rid of him, 'Just go!' and heaving with all his might he got most of Catweazle out of the window. For a moment he hung on the sill, then with a final shove and a crash of broken glass Catweazle fell out into the night.

Sam finally pushed the chair away from the door and staggered into the room just as Mr Bennet, hearing the noise of breaking glass, came hurrying in from the scullery.

'What the devil are you two up to?' he said angrily.

'*Me*, boss!' said Sam with outraged innocence, as Carrot finally managed to close the shattered window.

'How did that happen, Carrot?' said Mr Bennet, pointing grimly at the window.

Carrot, deciding to tell his father everything, opened his mouth to speak.

'Well, you see, Dad,' he began. 'There was this – ', but he found he couldn't say any more. His voice just wouldn't come. He tried again. 'There was this – ', but it was no good, he had dried up completely.

'Well, come on,' said his father patiently, 'tell me.'

Carrot tried again, but it was impossible for him to say anything at all about Catweazle.

'I can't,' he said desperately.

'What d'you mean – you can't?' Mr Bennet was beginning to lose his temper.

'Well,' said Carrot, 'I want to, but – ', and again he found it impossible to speak. With a great effort Mr Bennet controlled himself.

'I'll give you one last chance to explain. Do you understand?'

'Yes, Dad,' said Carrot, preparing himself.

'Good. Now what exactly have you been up to?'

Carrot opened his mouth but no sound came out. He pointed to his mouth, then to the window and sadly shook his head.

'All right,' said Mr Bennet furiously. 'If you're going to play about with me, my lad, you'd better go straight to bed!'

Carrot walked miserably across the room and turning at the door, made one last attempt to speak.

'Go to bed!' ordered his father, convinced that Carrot was just trying to be funny, and the boy slunk out of the room.

'Ain't never seen 'im like that before,' said Sam. Mr Bennet sighed heavily. 'When I was in the army,' he said, 'we called that dumb insolence.'

There was a sudden gobbling from one of the turkey pens. The two men listened.

'Could be a fox,' said Sam.

It wasn't a fox. It was Catweazle looking for somewhere to hide for the night. He shied away from the strange birds and their unearthly cries and eventually found refuge in a disused chicken coop, on the edge of the farm. Creeping in and carefully shutting the door behind him, he examined his new shelter.

Hanging from the roof was an old hurricane lantern, so Catweazle looked on the door post for a switch. As chance would have it there was a large nail sticking out at an angle, and he crooked his finger round it and looking towards the lantern, gave a tug.

'Shine tiny sun,' he chanted, pulling on the nail. 'Shine tiny sun!' Nothing happened. There was no blinding light to dazzle him and after trying again for a few times he gave up.

He settled himself in the hay, bewildered by all the extraordinary happenings. He had jumped forward through time nine hundred years, of this there was no doubt, and now he found himself in a world of new and powerful magic.

'On the morrow, I will ask the young sorcerer many things. Mayhap he will teach me the new magic, for I have much to learn.' And with this considerable understatement, he fell asleep.

3

CASTLE SABURAC

CATWEAZLE woke very early the next morning hearing a strange noise in the sky. The hair stood up on his dirty neck as it came nearer, and finally, when the thunderous noise was overhead he could bear it no longer, and, darting out of the chicken coop he looked up and saw a huge fish swimming across the sky. Its fins were motionless, and it roared so loudly that the earth shook.

As it passed over him, Catweazle flung himself down in the wet grass and waited for it to pounce, but the giant creature was apparently not hungry and it continued on its way until it disappeared in the distance. It was Catweazle's first aeroplane.

He rose unsteadily and began to creep towards the farm, hiding quickly as he saw Mr Bennet and Winston moving between the sheds. Still shaken by the aeroplane, he was making his way along the wall of the garage when he heard another strange sound, this time like the hissing of serpents. Curiosity overcoming his fear, he looked round the open door.

It was Barakiel! The Prince of Lightning! As the Demon turned his great head, revealing his one monstrous eye, showers of little stars tumbled from his blasting rod.

Catweazle jerked back making tiny cries of fear and a curious fizzing noise through his teeth. He turned and fled from the garage.

Sam Woodyard turned off the welder, and, lifting his protective helmet, caught a glimpse of Catweazle running towards the back door of the farmhouse.

Carrot, who was at the sink in the scullery, suddenly

saw Catweazle coming up to the house and quickly pulled the old man inside. Catweazle was in such a panic of fear that he ran past Carrot into the kitchen and went to earth under the table.

'Oh, Master, Master,' he moaned as Carrot ran in after him, 'deliver me from the Demon.' Getting a lump of chalk from a pocket in his tattered robe, he drew a circle round himself on the flagstones.

'Sator, Arepo, Tenet, Opera, Rotas,' he muttered.

'Get up,' said Carrot, who was expecting his father at any moment.

'Gab, gaba, agaba.'

'Will you get up?' ordered the boy, hauling him out. 'You've got me into enough trouble already. If Dad finds you, he'll skin you alive.'

Then the kettle whistled in the scullery and Catweazle, with another moan, dived under the table again.

' 'Tis the Demon!' he cried.

'It's the kettle, you fool,' said Carrot crossly, running into the scullery and turning off the gas. Slowly Catweazle came out from under the table.

'The kettle?' he said. 'It screams like a mandrake.'

'I thought you'd gone,' interrupted Carrot. 'What on earth made you come back?'

'Thy magic, O Master. Teach me thy magic and I will serve thee,' and once more the old man knelt in front of him.

The scullery door suddenly opened. Carrot left Catweazle and ran back into the scullery, shutting the kitchen door behind him as Mr Bennet shooed away Winston and came in from the yard.

'Hullo Dad,' said Carrot, rather overdoing it.

'What's up?' asked Mr Bennet suspiciously as he went over to the sink to wash.

'Nothing Dad,' said Carrot, busily making the tea.

'Haven't broken another window have you?'

'No Dad.'

'Well I'm glad you've got your voice back,' said his father, opening the kitchen door.

There was no sign of Catweazle. Carrot couldn't understand it. As Mr Bennet sat down at the table, he unwittingly put his feet in the magician's protective circle.

'Breakfast?' asked Carrot, suddenly noticing the ring of chalk.

' 'Fraid I've only time for a cuppa.'

Carrot rushed out to the scullery again. Picking up the tea-pot, he collected a dish cloth and then nearly bumped into Theda Watkins, the 'occasional help', as Mr Bennet described her, as she came in from the yard.

'Hey, steady, Carrot,' said Theda, warding off the tea-pot.

'Sorry, Theda,' he gasped as he tore back into the kitchen.

'Good man,' said his father, as he brought the tea.

Disappearing beneath the table, somewhat to Mr Bennet's surprise, Carrot quickly wiped the chalk circle from the floor. 'Spilt some milk,' he explained, surfacing again and looking round for traces of Catweazle.

'It's in here now!' said his father sniffing.

'What is?'

'That smell from the barn. Wonder if the drains are all right?'

Theda came in, tying on an apron. ' 'Mornin', Mr Bennet,' she said cheerfully. 'Ooh, who did that?' Mr Bennet followed her glance to the broken window.

'He did,' he said curtly, nodding at Carrot. 'That comes out of your pocket money, my lad,' he said, pulling on his boots again to go back to the turkeys.

Theda smiled at Carrot, as if to say 'never mind' and began sorting through a large pile of dirty washing on the scullery floor.

Where was Catweazle? He hadn't left the house, Carrot was sure of that. He sniffed his way out into the hall and then, with growing conviction, up the stairs. On the landing he paused, listening. The grandfather clock ticked in the hall below and in the distance he could hear the faint gobbling of the turkeys. Sniffing his way into his bedroom, he crossed to the wardrobe and threw it open. Inside, between Carrot's school blazer and his duffle coat, Catweazle stood like a ragged sentry.

'By what magic didst thou find me?' he gasped.

'I followed my nose,' said Carrot. 'Come out.'

Catweazle pushed his way out, looking even dirtier than before, while a few wire hangers clattered down behind him.

'Where did you sleep?' asked Carrot. Catweazle explained about the hen-house. 'I thought they'd pulled that down,' said Carrot, wondering how he was going to get rid of him.

'I don't know why I couldn't tell Dad about you last night,' he said. 'I tried to.'

'Thou hast sworn, remember?' Catweazle waved Adamcos at him. ' 'Tis my magic. Show me thine, thy ... electrickery, O master.'

'Oh, all right,' said Carrot, 'but you'll have to go then, O.K.?'

There was a pull-cord by the bed which operated a reading light on the head-board. After pulling it a few times, and then letting Catweazle have a go, Carrot carefully took out the bulb and handed it, still warm, to Catweazle. He took it gingerly and examined it.

' 'Tis a wonder, truly,' he whispered, feeling the rounded smoothness of the glass. 'And like a feather,' he added. He held it away from himself and pulled the cord with his other hand, very disappointed when nothing happened.

'Shine, tiny sun,' he said hopefully to the light bulb. 'Salmay, Dalmay, Adonay.'

'It's got to go in there,' said Carrot, taking it from him and pointing to the lamp socket.

'Where?' said Catweazle approaching the head-board.

'There,' said Carrot.

'There?' said Catweazle, jabbing his finger into the socket and touching the live terminals. With a loud cry, he fell backwards and collapsed in a little heap on the floor.

'Are you all right?' Carrot asked anxiously, getting down beside him.

'Oh! Oh! Oh! Oh!' cried Catweazle.

'You've had a shock,' explained Carrot.

'Indeed, indeed!' groaned the magician, keeping his face in the rug. 'Has it gone?'

'Has what gone?'

'The invisible horse that kicked me.'

Carrot rocked with laughter and Catweazle, realizing that the danger had passed, sat up on the floor, scratching himself, and looking angrily at the young magician who was making such a fool of him.

'I need thy magic,' he snapped.

'You need a bath,' said Carrot. Catweazle, who had no idea what a bath was, looked questioningly at the boy.

'I wonder if I dare,' murmured Carrot, thinking what fun it would be to clean him up.

'I do not like thy look,' said Catweazle uneasily.

'Come on,' said Carrot, making up his mind and leading Catweazle towards the bathroom.

In the garage, Sam was putting away his welding gear, when Mr Bennet came in for a can of oil.

'What did the old feller want, Boss?' asked Sam.

'What old fellow?' said Mr Bennet, examining the harrow Sam had just repaired.

'The old tramp Carrot took in.'

Mr Bennet looked at his foreman. 'What are you talking about? Carrot has had strict instructions not to feed any more tramps. There's no one in the house with him except Theda. Now, I'd like you to mend that window next and then take down that old hen-coop in Top Field. That job's been hanging fire for months.'

Before Sam could open his mouth to reply, Mr Bennet had collected the oil-can and strode out of the garage.

Wonder what's biting him, Sam thought. He *had* seen someone, he was sure of it. He took a dusty sheet of glass from a shelf at the back of the garage, and went up to the house. Theda was busy doing the washing when Sam came up to talk to her through the open scullery window. He was a bit soft about Theda.

' 'Mornin' Theda,' said Sam. 'Has the old tramp gone?' he added casually.

'What old tramp?' said Theda, up to her elbows in suds.

'Come off it,' said Sam. 'Carrot took him in. Dressed funny he was. Like an old monk.'

'You're seein' things,' said Theda, washing away.

Upstairs, Carrot hummed purposefully as he ran the water into the bath.

'Shut the door,' he ordered Catweazle who was wandering around examining everything with childlike wonder. The lavatory chain fascinated him and, waving his other arm hopefully at the light bulb, he pulled. The cistern flushed loudly and Catweazle, terrified, made for the door. Carrot, however, beat him to it and shot the bolt. Then he pushed Catweazle towards the bath. The old man made his strange fizzing sounds of alarm.

'Nay, kill me not,' he pleaded, once more going down on his knees.

'Take it off,' said Carrot firmly, pointing to the old man's robe.

Catweazle looked at the bath then up at the boy, suddenly realizing the fate in store for him. 'No – no! Not in the water! Do not put me in the water – I shall drown.'

'Don't be daft,' said Carrot heartlessly. 'Get in.'

'Thou legless lizard! Thou wriggling grub! Thou soft-backed beetle!' cursed Catweazle in impotent fury.

'No good calling me names,' said Carrot. 'Get in.' The boy was implacable. Holding up his robe and still wearing his home-made rabbit-skin boots, Catweazle cautiously put both feet in the bath. As the hot water soaked through to his feet, he gave a howl and jumped out.

'It burns! It burns!' he moaned, running round the bathroom in little desperate circles.

'Will you shut up!' said Carrot, swishing in more cold water.

'When I escape, I shall cast such a spell – ' the magician threatened.

'Back you get,' said Carrot calmly.

Seeing there was no escape, the old man climbed back in and stood miserably eyeing the bath water as he took off his robe. Then he lost his balance on the slippery bath and his feet shot from under him, water going in all directions.

In the scullery, Theda heard the splash and looked up. 'He'll use all the hot water,' she thought to herself, surprised at Carrot having a bath without being told.

Carrot soaped Catweazle busily. It was rather like washing Winston. The old man sat, utterly defeated, as the dirt ran off him and the water turned a nasty grey.

'Here – you do it,' said Carrot, handing him the soap. 'I'll get a towel. Don't go away,' and he left Catweazle covered in soap and wishing he was dead.

Carrot took a towel from the airing cupboard on the landing and was just going back to Catweazle when Theda came up the stairs and caught him at the bathroom door.

'I thought you was in the bath?' she said.

'That's right,' said Carrot breathlessly, 'I am ... er ... was, I mean.' A tremendous splash came from inside the bathroom where Catweazle, hearing Theda's voice had attempted, unsuccessfully, to get out of the bath.

With a surprised look at Carrot, Theda pushed past him and opened the bathroom door.

Catweazle stood in the bath wearing the bath-mat round his skinny middle. Round his neck hung Adamcos in its sheath. With a piercing shriek, Theda began to have hysterics while Catweazle climbed out of the bath and began to advance on her.

'Out woman! Out!' he cried, drawing Adamcos. 'Lest I turn thee into a one-legged ferret!'

Seeing the knife, Theda backed against the wall, convinced she was about to be murdered.

'Know that I am Catweazle,' he intoned, waving Adamcos before her terrified eyes. 'Master of the Black Arts, Follower of the Secret Path,' and he began to mutter a spell, 'Zazel, Hasmael, Barsabel, Betharshesim, Shedbarshemoth, Hasmoday.'

Slowly Theda's eyes began to close as they followed the moving knife and Carrot, watching from the door, realized with amazement that Catweazle was hypnotizing her. He remembered his own experience of the moving knife and how those glittering eyes had bored into his own the previous night.

'I don the cloak of darkness,' intoned the magician. 'When thou wakest, thou shalt not see me. Invisible ... invisible ... invisible ...'

'Invisible ... invisible ... invisible ...' repeated Theda with her eyes firmly closed.

' 'Tis done,' said Catweazle. 'Now thou canst wake,' and he snapped his fingers and blew on her face.

'Wake!' he commanded. Theda's eyes popped open. She looked straight through Catweazle as if he wasn't there and then turned to Carrot.

'Anything you want washing?' she asked calmly, and went to look in the clothes bin.

'Fantastic,' breathed Carrot, as Theda left with a bundle of washing.

Catweazle was pleased. He had impressed the young magician.

'I too have the Power,' he said proudly.

'How long will she stay like that?'

'At sunset the Power will fade.'

'Can you hypnotize anyone? Er – you know, what you call the Power?' Carrot asked excitedly. The old man gave an enigmatic smile.

'We will do many things, thou and I. I will summon up Spirits to ride thy invisible horses.' He paused. 'Would that Touchwood were here,' he said sadly. And then seeing the boy's puzzled expression, 'My familiar,' he added, 'in that ... other time.'

Carrot, who didn't want to start him talking about the Normans again, looked round for the robe. It was nowhere to be seen. Suddenly they both realized what had happened: Theda had taken it. She was going to wash it! They looked at each other in horror.

'We'll have to wait until she hangs it out,' said Carrot. 'Come on.'

They sneaked downstairs and out through the front door. Taking refuge in the gooseberry bushes they waited for Theda to bring the washing to the clothes-line.

After what seemed like hours, Theda came staggering out with the wet things and began pegging them out. Sam, who had finished mending the window, strolled over to talk to her just as she took Catweazle's robe from the wicker basket and began to hang it on the line. The sight of this infuriated Catweazle.

' 'Tis mine! And I will have it!' he muttered, as Carrot frantically tried to restrain him.

'Sam'll see you!' he warned.

'Unhand me, thou acorn,' said Catweazle savagely as he rose out of the bushes and charged towards the clothes-line.

Sam looked in terror at the apparition running across the lawn at him. He couldn't move. His mouth opened and closed like a fish. Theda, to whom Catweazle was still invisible, went on unconcernedly pegging out the clothes as the old man reached the line, snatched his robe from it, and ran off through the bushes.

'I will see thee at the little house,' he hissed at Carrot as he scampered past their hiding-place.

For a moment Sam stood, stuttering incoherently. 'The old monk!' he finally managed to gasp.

'Eh?' said Theda, turning to him with a clothes peg in her mouth.

'The old monk! The old monk!'

Theda stared at him with alarm. She had never seen him so excited.

'He didn't have anythin' on!' Sam continued, gesticulating wildly in the direction of the gooseberry bushes. Theda, convinced that Sam had gone mad, dropped the washing and ran off round the house calling to Mr Bennet.

Sam sat down shakily on an old box and tried to recover. He glanced round nervously. He had seen *something*, he was sure of that, and nothing anyone could say was going to change his mind.

Carrot watched from the bushes as Theda came running back with his father.

'Now Sam,' said Mr Bennet, hurrying up, 'what's the matter? Been at the cider again?'

Sam sighed. 'Look Mr Bennet,' he said, 'I ain't makin' of it up. There's an old feller runnin' round this here farm stark naked.'

'All right Sam,' said Mr Bennet. 'If I see him, I'll tell him to go away.'

'You think I'm seein' things, don't you?' said Sam angrily.

'I'm sure of it.'

'But you was with me, Theda,' he pleaded, looking up at her.

Theda and Mr Bennet exchanged a glance.

'Listen, Sam, you've had some sort of hallucination if you ask me. Now you don't want to worry about it. Just try to forget it. Lots of people see things.'

Sam stared at him. 'But he looked so real!' he said.

'Oh, he would,' agreed Mr Bennet. There was a silence while Sam thought about it. A hallucination? Was that what he'd seen? One in the yard with clothes on, and one on the lawn with no clothes on?

'I'm sorry I've held things up, boss,' he said finally. 'But I ain't never seen a hallucination before.' He got to his feet. 'I'll go an' work it off on somethin'. Nothin' like hard work for clearin' yer head.'

'Good man,' said Mr Bennet with considerable relief.

'What about knocking that old hen-house down?'

'Right, boss,' said Sam with determination.

From the bushes, Carrot watched with horror as Sam set off with a large axe over his shoulder. There was nothing the boy could do to stop him so, keeping out of sight, he followed Sam up to the hen house which stood rotting away in the corner of Top Field.

Sam tried the door but it wouldn't open because Catweazle had tied it shut with a piece of twine. 'That's funny,' muttered Sam, tugging at the handle. Hearing Sam outside, Catweazle struggled into his damp robe as quickly as he could. Sam pulled harder and as the twine finally snapped, he staggered back and sat down.

Catweazle poked his head out of the door and the two of them stared at each other.

'I'm nuts,' muttered Sam unhappily. 'I ought to be locked up.'

'I am invisible, invisible,' quavered Catweazle, waving Adamcos.

'I wish you was,' groaned Sam getting unsteadily to his feet.

'Sator, Arepo, Tenet, Opera, Rotas,' Catweazle went on but Sam suddenly leant forward and touched him. At this Catweazle's nerve deserted him, and he ran back into the shed and shut the door.

'You're real,' roared Sam. 'You ain't no hallucination!' and he shook the hen-coop furiously. Catweazle held grimly to the handle as the shed began to disintegrate around him. Finally in the face of Sam's onslaught the whole thing collapsed like a pack of cards. For a moment Catweazle stood amidst the wreckage, still clutching the handle, while Sam thrashed about under the door, then with a howl he turned and ran into the wood behind him.

'I'll get you, you old devil,' said Sam, as he crawled out from under the door. Brandishing his axe, he set off in pursuit, with Carrot once again following some way behind, but Catweazle just melted into the wood and search as he might Sam couldn't find him. He searched with less and less hope till eventually he gave up, satisfied at least that he had frightened the 'hallucination' away from the farm forever. There were certain questions he wanted to ask Carrot, he thought to himself as he shouldered the axe and made his way back to the farm.

Carrot continued to search. He felt worried about the old man. 'Catweazle,' he called. 'It's me. Where are you?' But there was no reply.

Carrot didn't give up easily. The wood was large, but he knew it well and presently he found himself near the Forestry Estate which joined his father's property. Years ago, during the war, there had been an army camp here. Now the only thing left was an old water tower covered in rusty barbed-wire and with a big 'Danger. W.D. Property' notice on the scaffolding.

'Well, that's that,' thought Carrot. 'He's gone.'

He was about to turn for home when Catweazle's head appeared at the top of the water tower.

'Here, boy,' he called down. Carrot looked up in astonishment. The old man waved a skinny arm at him.

'How did you get up there?' called Carrot.

'I climbed,' said Catweazle.

'You can't live in that!'

'Why not?'

'It's full of water.'

'Nay, boy,' the old man shook his head, ' 'tis empty.'

'Are you sure?' said Carrot.

'Come and see,' beckoned Catweazle.

'But it belongs to the army –'

'I see no soldiers,' replied Catweazle, looking round. ' 'Tis my castle now.'

'But Dad says it isn't safe,' said Carrot, remembering his father saying he was never to climb it.

44

DANGER
W.D. PROPERTY

'No arrow could pierce it,' said Catweazle, confidently banging at the rusty steel tank. 'Come up.'

Carrot could see that Catweazle had managed to pull the barbed-wire away from the iron ladder, and setting his feet on the rungs he began to climb. The ladder creaked as he climbed and Catweazle held out his arm to help him as he reached the top.

'Thanks,' said Carrot.

'Follow me,' said Catweazle and descended the inspection hole.

Carrot followed. It was like going into a submarine. As his eyes got used to the dim light inside the tank, Carrot could see that he was in a steel box with small girder-like struts at angles to the walls. It was indeed empty except for dead leaves that had blown in through the open inspection hole. Light filtered in through cracks between the steel plates and the whole place was festooned with thick cobwebs.

'Welcome,' said Catweazle, his voice echoing impressively round the tank.

'This is super!' said Carrot, wishing he'd found it first.

'Saburac, one of the Spirits of the Brazen Vessel, led me here,' said Catweazle.

'Oh, did he?'

'In his honour, I have named it Castle Saburac, for 'tis a magic place.'

'Castle Saburac,' said Carrot relishing the strange word. 'It's terrific!'

Catweazle came closer to him. In the half light, he looked very mysterious. 'But wonder upon wonders! Another lives here!' he said.

Carrot looked round uneasily. 'Another what?' he said.

'My Spirits have brought him,' said Catweazle happily. 'Now my magic is assured. We will work together, he and I. And thou, boy!' Catweazle held out his hand. In it was a large greeny-brown toad.

'See!' said Catweazle with triumph and pride. ' 'Tis my familiar, Touchwood!'

4

THE CURSE OF RAPKYN

ONE morning at breakfast Mr Bennet looked up from a rude letter from his bank manager, to find Carrot trying to feed a tortoise with a slice of banana.

'What on earth's that thing doing on the table?' he asked.

Carrot, who had been hiding the tortoise behind the tea-cosy, quickly put it on the floor.

'I was only getting it used to me,' he said, 'Sam brought him for me. His name's Beelzebub. He's my familiar.'

'Your what?' said his father.

'My familiar,' said Carrot. 'Witches and wizards had them. They were sort of pets. I read all about them in this book.'

'*Magic through the Ages*,' read Mr Bennet. 'So that's the latest craze is it?'

'It's jolly interesting.'

'Hmm – I wish it worked. I'd get you to put a spell on Winkley.'

'Who's he?'

'My bank manager.' Mr Bennet tapped the letter, 'I've got to see him this afternoon about my over-draft.'

Carrot was just going to ask him what an overdraft was, when Sam came in looking very harassed. 'You'd better come, boss,' he said, 'I've just culled twenty-three birds. It's sinovitis again.'

'Oh Lord!' groaned Mr Bennet, getting up from the table, 'I'm beginning to think there's a curse on this place.'

'A curse!' said Carrot excitedly.

'We've got a budding wizard in the family, Sam,' Mr Bennet explained as they hurried out, 'for this week anyway.'

Carrot searched through his book. ' "The power of the Evil Eye",' he read eagerly, ' "Secret names were used to call up demons to destroy one's enemies." ' He picked up Beelzebub, who stuck his head quickly back inside his shell. 'Come on Beelzy! I bet Catweazle knows all about curses. Let's go and ask him!'

Leaving the farm, Carrot ran across the fields, carrying Beelzebub and some provisions for Catweazle in his rucksack. He had been to the water tank several times since the old man had made his home there, usually taking him food and bottles of milk.

As he reached the top of the ladder he could hear Catweazle muttering to himself inside:

> 'Hob-hole hob, Hob-hole hob.
> Tak't off, tak't off.
> Old one, cold one,
> Cure my bone-ache.'

Carrot took off his rucksack, eased himself through the inspection hole and climbed down into the tank. ' 'Morning, Catweazle,' he said.

Catweazle paused, about to drink from an old baked-bean tin while Touchwood looked on beadily.

'What have you got there?' asked Carrot, looking at the nasty mess in the tin.

'A potion for bone-ache,' said the old man. 'I forgot the earwigs,' he added. Carrot sniffed the revolting mixture. 'I think I'd rather have bone-ache,' he said.

'Would that I had my book,' Catweazle muttered.

'I've got one,' said Carrot, producing *Magic through the Ages*. Catweazle grabbed it eagerly. He looked blankly at the pages, and tried turning it upside down, but he still couldn't read it, so he gave it back to Carrot.

' 'Tis in thy magic writing,' he said, 'not mine.'

Carrot carefully took Beelzebub from the rucksack and held him up. 'Meet my familiar,' he said.

Catweazle fizzed in sudden alarm. 'A stone with legs!' he cried.

'His name's Beelzebub,' said Carrot, putting the tortoise down next to Touchwood, who eyed him suspiciously. 'Here, have a banana.'

Catweazle took the curved yellow thing from the boy, holding it carefully in case it was dangerous.

'You eat it,' said Carrot. 'But you peel it first!' he added quickly, as Catweazle prepared to take a bite.

Carrot peeled back a strip of the skin, but before he could stop him, Catweazle pulled it from the banana and started to chew it greedily.

'Not that bit!' said Carrot, 'the middle bit.'

Catweazle ate the banana in silence. He enjoyed it tremendously.

'You seem to be settling in all right,' said Carrot, handing him the rest of the bunch.

'Ay, boy. Last night I found some sacks.'

'Where?'

'In thy barn,' Catweazle leered, and peeled another banana. Carrot was very indignant. 'We've got enough trouble without you stealing,' he said. 'Dad's got an overdraft.'

'Over draft?'

'It's something to do with money.'

'Money?'

Carrot sighed. 'It's jolly difficult even to talk to you sometimes. The farm's had a lot of bad luck, you see. Dad thinks there's a curse on the place.'

'Most like. Most like,' said Catweazle, gobbling the banana.

'D'you know anything about curses?'

'Saucey snail! I know everything about curses. There is

50

a curse for everything. They were all in my book,' he said bitterly.

'If the farm was cursed, could you uncurse it?'

'Ay, if I knew the curse.'

'Like poisons and antidotes you mean?'

There was silence while Carrot thought hard. Finding the curse was not going to be easy, especially as he had no idea where to start.

'Stuffy!' he cried suddenly. Catweazle jumped and then crossed his fingers in case the boy was beginning a spell. 'Stuffy Gladstone,' Carrot explained. 'He runs the museum; he's the curate or something. He came to the school and bored us stiff about local history.' Catweazle kept his fingers firmly crossed. What was the young sorcerer talking about?

'If Hexwood's got a curse on it, Stuffy'll know about it. Anyway I bet he can look it up. That place is full of old books. Look after Beelzy, I'll be back.'

Climbing down the water tower, Carrot set off across the Forestry Estate towards Old Westbourne House, an ugly Jacobean mansion, part of which contained the Westbourne and District Folk Museum. What he didn't know was that Catweazle was following some way behind him, drawn by the mention of old books.

As Carrot disappeared round a sharp bend, Catweazle stopped to examine the huge magic letters that some sorcerer had painted on the road. He had never seen a 'Slow' sign before, and he couldn't read it anyway. He knelt down on the road and traced the shape of the giant 'S'. ' 'Tis a serpent,' he muttered and then as he became aware of a threatening noise behind him he glanced round. His eyes widened with fear. Racing down the road was a snarling, scarlet monster. It bore down on him, hooting and roaring, and he dived into the ditch as the red sports car shot past and skidded round the bend.

Catweazle waited some time before he crawled shakily from the muddy ditch, and as he did so he heard another car coming. 'It hath my scent,' he muttered, 'I cannot escape,' and once more he dived into the ditch.

Apollo Twelve, with Sam Woodyard driving it, came rattling round the bend. Clouds of black smoke poured from the exhaust pipe as the old car shook its way along the road. In his imagination, Sam was battling his way round the tricky bends of the Zandvoort circuit in Holland, with a tenacious Italian driver on his tail. In reality he was going to get some chicken wire to repair the fence.

Catweazle watched his enemy drive past. 'Faster than the wild boar,' he muttered, 'and men sit inside!' He was in a world peopled with sorcerers. Now all men followed the magic path.

He rose from the ditch as a third car came by. The driver hooted at him, thinking he was about to cross.

'Blow your trumpets, my brothers!' he called after the car as he set off to catch up with the boy.

Carrot had reached Westbourne House by now. Inside

the main hall an arrow pointed the way to the Folk Museum. As he went in, Carrot saw the small weedy figure of Mr Gladstone, standing in front of a party of strawhatted schoolgirls.

'Cernunnos, the Romans called him,' droned Stuffy, pointing to a primitive little stone statue on a plinth beside him. 'Incomplete, I'm afraid. Originally he had two heads, like Janus, you know.'

'Who's Janus, Miss Arthur?' one of the girls asked the teacher in charge of the party. 'Ssh, Daphne,' said Miss Arthur, who was the games mistress.

'We're lucky to see Cernunnos at all,' Stuffy ploughed on. 'Although he was originally found near here, he lives at the British Museum. Professor Honnerton arranged the loan and he's coming today to collect our friend.'

'Well, thank you, Mr Gladstone,' Miss Arthur interrupted neatly. 'May we ...?' and she indicated the other rooms.

'Do, do,' said Stuffy. 'If there's anything else I can illuminate ...'

Miss Arthur and the girls began wandering off as Carrot came up to Stuffy. 'Excuse me, Mr Gladstone,' he said.

'Yes?'

'I wonder if you can help me. I'm Edward Bennet and I live at Hexwood Turkey Farm –'

'Hexwood? Oh yes, partly seventeenth century. Nice old place.'

'Hasn't got a curse on it, has it?' asked Carrot.

Before Stuffy could reply, there was a loud crash from the entrance hall. Catweazle, having tracked Carrot to the museum, had just come face to face with the figure of a Norman soldier, complete with helmet and chain mail. Puzzled by its failure to attack him, he had kicked it hard on the shins, bringing it toppling to the ground. As Carrot and Stuffy came running out, Catweazle put one foot on the prone figure.

'Death to the invader!' he shouted in triumph.

'Good gracious!' said Stuffy, as the schoolgirls ran up from the other rooms. 'What happened? Did you touch the exhibit?'

'I'm sure he didn't, Mr Gladstone,' said Carrot, glaring at Catweazle.

'Do you know this . . . er . . . gentleman?' asked Stuffy.

'Yes,' said Carrot. 'He's staying at the farm with us, aren't you, Mr . . . er . . . Brown?'

'Oh, I see,' said Stuffy uncertainly, looking at the ragged figure.

Together, Carrot and he managed to lift the Norman soldier back into position.

'There, that's better,' said Stuffy, dusting it down. 'No damage done. After all, he was meant to be biffed about a bit, wasn't he, Mr Brown?' and he looked around for Catweazle, who had drifted into the museum.

'He's gone inside,' said Carrot.

'Oh, has he? He's a bit odd, isn't he? Why does he wear that . . . thing?'

'I dunno. He's worn it for years.'

Inside, Catweazle suddenly began whistling.

'What's he doing now?' Stuffy asked nervously as they hurried in. Watched by the schoolgirls and Miss Arthur, Catweazle was crawling across the floor between the glass cases.

'What are you up to?' whispered Carrot, crouching down beside him.

'I have lost him again.'

'You didn't bring Touchwood, did you?'

'He wanted to come.'

'You'll get us thrown out! He thinks you're potty anyway.'

As Stuffy came up to them, Catweazle crawled away again, calling and whistling. 'Come boy – come. Come, my merry boy!'

Stuffy turned to Carrot. 'He really is very odd, isn't he? What's he think he's lost?'

There was a shriek from Miss Arthur.

'I think he's found it,' said Carrot.

The schoolgirls were staring at Touchwood, who had crawled on to Miss Arthur's shoe and was trying hard to make himself comfortable. Regaining an iron control, Miss Arthur shook the toad off her foot and stalked out angrily, followed by the giggling girls. Catweazle picked up his familiar and put him carefully in his pocket.

'Ugh – a toad!' said Stuffy, drawing back sharply, as Catweazle went over to the little statue of Cernunnos.

'Cernunnos,' he said, blowing on his thumb-ring, 'cast not thine evil eye on me. Terfita, Estamos, Perfiter!'

'Good heavens,' exclaimed Stuffy. 'How does he know it's Cernunnos?' he asked.

'Er . . . what about the farm?' said Carrot quickly. 'You know, Hexwood?'

'Oh, yes,' said Stuffy, 'I was forgetting. We'd better try Flint's *Survey of Westbourne 1720*,' and he climbed a tall step-ladder to search among the shelves of dusty old books.

'Here we are,' he said, pulling one out. 'Not much, I'm afraid. "The new house at Hexwood is of most pleasant aspect. One Rapkyn, 'tis said, bound all who live there in turmoil, but such matter is for the foolish." That's all there is on Hexwood.'

' "Bound all who live there in turmoil",' repeated Carrot. 'What does it mean?'

'Tobias Flint is often very obscure,' said Stuffy, replacing the book and coming down the ladder.

'Thou flibbertigibbet,' cried Catweazle, who had been listening, 'all is clear as spring water. This Rapkyn was a sorcerer!'

'Really, Mr Brown,' said Stuffy, 'how can you possibly know that?' But Catweazle just pushed past him and climbed swiftly up the ladder with Adamcos held in front of him like a torch.

'Mr Brown,' said Stuffy, 'I'd rather you didn't. ...' A book came sailing down and bounced off his head. It was followed by others, as Catweazle searched frantically through the shelves. He could feel by the tingling in his arm that there was a magic book somewhere and he was going to find it. Clouds of dust began to rise and the books continued to fall.

Stuffy was furious. 'Come down, Brown!' he ordered. 'Will you stop it!'

The books stopped raining down. Catweazle had found what he wanted; he stood above them, clasping a tattered old book with a look of wild excitement.

'True magic!' he yelled, shinning down the ladder and skipping round the museum. Reaching the doorway, he held the book over his head. 'The Power is within!' he cried, ' 'tis Rapkyn's book!' and with a final blood-curdling cry of triumph, he turned and scampered out.

Slowly, Stuffy Gladstone collapsed on the bottom step of the ladder and looked at the pile of books scattered around him, unable to speak.

'Don't worry, Mr Gladstone,' said Carrot, 'I'll get it back,' but it was some time before he found Catweazle sitting on a gate and reading from the stolen book.

'Come on, hand it over,' panted Carrot.

'It stays with me,' said the old magician, gripping the book in his claw-like hands and running off into the field.

'Listen,' said Carrot, catching up with him, 'it's not yours. You've just got to give it back.'

'Cross me not,' snapped Catweazle, 'I have found thy curse.'

'What!'

Catweazle put a finger to his lips, twisted his thin beard and led the way over to a hay-stack. They sat down like a pair of conspirators and Catweazle opened the book. Carrot looked over his shoulder at the curious spider-like squiggles. 'What's it say?' he asked.

'Hear Rapkyn!' said Catweazle.

> ' "Hexwood, I blight thee,
> Stones hold my power.
> One in the water,
> One in the tower." '

Carrot was mystified. 'I'm sorry, but I don't get it,' he said.

'Thou mugwump! "Stones hold my power!" '

'What stones?'

'The stones Rapkyn cursed and then hid,' said Catweazle impatiently.

'Why did he do that?'

Catweazle looked at the boy. Was he really stupid or just pretending?

'Hexwood. "Hex" wood,' he said slowly. 'Hex meaneth witch, thou maggot! The wood was a meeting place for witches and when the house was built, this Rapkyn took revenge.'

Carrot jumped up. 'You mean we've got to find a couple of stones buried somewhere in the farm?'

'Truly, thou art Solomon,' said Catweazle sarcastically.

There was no one about when they got back to the farm, and after Carrot had made sure that it was quite safe, the two of them crept into the kitchen. There was a note for Carrot propped up against a milk bottle on the table.

' "Gone to see Winkley. Back at four." ' he read, 'That means we've only got an hour!'

Catweazle had sat himself down and was eagerly reading the book again.

' 'Tis all here!' he muttered to himself, 'Prayers to

Tanit, prayers to Lucifer, spells, charms, and curses!'

'We're going to have to work fast,' said Carrot. ' "One in the water, one in the tower", but we haven't got a tower, so what can it mean? "One in the tower," ' and he put his chin in his hands and sat down to puzzle it out. Then his eye fell on the large chimney breast with the row of pewter beer mugs along the great oak beam. It was the oldest part of the house.

'The chimney!' he breathed. 'Could old Rapkyn mean the chimney? He must; it's the only tower we've got. Gosh, if it's up there, we'll never find it.'

'We will try,' said Catweazle.

Carrot ran and fetched some steps from the scullery and, moving the electric fire out of the way, set them up under the open chimney. They looked up the black tunnel above them.

'Right,' said Carrot, 'up you go.' Catweazle drew back, shaking his head.

'Go on! It's all right. There's no soot.'

'There may be Demons!'

'Think so? Then you hold the ladder,' and Carrot began to climb up the chimney. He had a small torch with him and he shone it over the rough stonework.

'What sort of stone am I looking for?' he called down to Catweazle.

' 'Twill have an eye.'

'A stone with an eye? What are you talking about?'

'Come down, thou cuckoo!' called Catweazle.

Carrot came down. 'We'll never find it,' he said, but Catweazle looked at him with contempt and, drawing Adamcos, climbed up into the blackness.

'Wouldn't you like the torch?' Carrot called. 'There's a sort of foothold if you want to go higher.'

There was no reply and presently a few loose bits of rubble began to fall as Catweazle searched in the darkness above.

'Do be careful,' said Carrot.

' 'Tis here!' a muffled voice said suddenly. 'I have found the stone!'

'Hang on,' said Carrot excitedly and he ran into the kitchen to fetch a hammer and chisel. He was still rummaging in the tool-box when Sam came in from the yard.

'Hullo, Carrot,' he said, 'where's the steps?'

'Er . . . I need them,' said Carrot.

'So do I,' said Sam seeing them in the chimney, and before Carrot could stop him, he picked them up and marched out.

'You'd better come down quick,' Carrot whispered up the chimney.

There was a rumbling noise, and Catweazle came crashing down into the fireplace. A moment later, he disappeared under an avalanche of soot.

'I didn't mean that quick,' said Carrot.

'No soot! No soot!' said Catweazle rising from the debris. 'I am like Shedbarshemoth, the black Demon of the moon.' He handed a lump of stone to Carrot. 'Here, take the accursed thing,' he said.

'You sure this is it?' asked Carrot.

Catweazle looked as if he might explode.

'All right,' said the boy quickly, 'let's give it a wash. Better give you one as well,' he added.

As they washed the stone at the sink, they could see Sam in the distance, repairing the fence on the other side of the yard.

'You're right,' said Carrot, rubbing off the dirt, 'It has got an eye.' The stone also had part of a nose and mouth too. Something about it was vaguely familiar. 'It's jolly old,' said Carrot.

'One in the water,' muttered the sooty figure beside him.

'In the water,' Carrot repeated. 'What does he mean by that?'

Catweazle's eyes shone through the grime on his face.

'Hast thou a well?' he said.

The well was on the far side of the house and no longer in use. Chicken-wire had been nailed over the top but the rusty chain was still round the roller. Tearing the wire away, Carrot looked in.

'Looks a long way down, but there's only mud at the bottom.' He turned to Catweazle, 'Sure you'll be all right?'

'*I* am not going down,' Catweazle said firmly. Carrot swung the bucket over the low wall, 'Climb in,' he said.

'Nay,' said Catweazle, 'I have the bone-ache.'

'What shall I turn you into?' said Carrot, looking thoughtfully at the magician.

'I will go! I will go!' said Catweazle, terrified of the young sorcerer.

While Carrot held the handle steady, Catweazle swung his legs over the low wall, and, hooking the bucket to the side, he managed to get both feet in it. Then, holding on to the chain, he swung out over the well as Carrot began to wind him down.

'Slowly! Thou devil's hiccup!' warned Catweazle as he descended. Carrot turned the handle more slowly, 'Seen anything yet?' he asked.

Catweazle's voice echoed up, 'Not yet,' he called. Carrot continued to lower the magician.

'Wait!' said Catweazle.

'What?' said Carrot and let go of the handle. With a great rattling it spun round as the rest of the chain paid out. There was a crash and then silence. Carrot was horrified.

'Catweazle!' he called, but there was no reply. 'Catweazle!!'

A croak came floating up from the bottom of the well.

'Touchwood!' asked Carrot anxiously, 'is he all right?'

'Thou maggot!' an infuriated voice replied, and Carrot breathed a sigh of relief. 'I thought you were dead,' he said.

A stream of abuse rose from the bottom of the well. It was obvious Catweazle had suffered no damage.

'Can you see the stone?' Carrot interrupted.

'Many little stars, but no stone.'

'Well it must be down there somewhere. Don't give up.'

There was a long silence from the bottom of the well and then finally Catweazle called once more, 'I am weary. Lift me up.'

'But we've got to find it, Catweazle.'

'I am cold, thou wood-louse. Lift me.'

'Oh, all right,' said Carrot, very disappointed. 'Get in the bucket.'

He began to haul him up. The chain creaked as Catweazle slowly came into view. He was dirtier than ever. As well as the dust from the museum and the soot from the chimney, he now had a liberal coating of mud. He climbed out of the bucket.

'Thou nettle-face!' he said. 'Wouldst plunge me to my death?'

'Sorry I let go like that,' said Carrot, 'but I thought you'd found it, you see.' Carrot sighed, 'Anyway, you tried.'

'Verily,' the old sorcerer nodded gravely. Then, delving into his robe and twisting his face into a wicked grin, he handed Carrot the second stone.

The two stones fitted together – like magic – and Carrot stared at the carved face in his hands, remembering where he had seen it before. Catweazle blew on his thumb-ring, ' 'Tis Cernunnos,' he said, fearfully.

*

Later in the museum Stuffy held the missing pieces against the statue of Cernunnos, his hands trembling with excitement.

'Incredible! Absolutely incredible! The statue is once more complete! Cernunnos has two heads again! This is a find in a million.'

'Well, it was really Mr Brown,' said Carrot. 'I haven't got the book back, I'm afraid,' he added.

'Oh keep it, keep it,' said Stuffy, examining the pieces through a magnifying glass. 'Just wait till old Honnerton gets here!'

Mr Bennet, who had been told by his bank manager that Head Office needed eight hundred pounds immediately, arrived home to find the kitchen covered in soot. It was the final blow in what was now, literally, a very black day.

When Carrot returned, his father was waiting for him.

'Look at this mess!' he stormed. 'When are you going to grow up and start behaving responsibly? What on earth have you been doing?'

Carrot sensed that things had gone badly at the bank. The curse was evidently still working, he thought gloomily.

'Your whole attitude is completely childish,' Mr Bennet went on, still smarting from his interview.

Carrot had just opened his mouth to reply when the phone rang in the hall and Mr Bennet went to answer it. It was Stuffy Gladstone. He was sorry to trouble Mr Bennet, he said, but Professor Honnerton had insisted that he phoned at once because of the value of the find.

'Find?' said Mr Bennet, bewildered, 'what find?'

'The missing pieces of Cernunnos,' Stuffy's precise voice replied. 'Your boy found them. I've got Honnerton with me and he says there's absolutely no doubt his department will make you an offer. Speaking off the cuff, I should say it will be in the region of eight hundred pounds.'

'What!' said Mr Bennet, almost dropping the phone.

'Possibly a bit more. All right to keep them here?'

'I suppose so,' said Mr Bennet, wondering if he was dreaming.

'You'll hear direct from the British Museum. Good-bye.'

Mr Bennet replaced the receiver and turned to Carrot. 'Eight hundred pounds? What on earth did you find, Carrot?'

Carrot smiled mysteriously at his father. Now he was sure that the curse had been removed. Perhaps Catweazle really was some sort of magician after all.

Back in Castle Saburac, Catweazle looked up from Rapkyn's book and winked at his familiar.

'This Rapkyn was a master, Touchwood. 'Tis all within these pages. This magic I can understand. Our way back lies here.'

And once more, he began to read.

5

THE MANNIKIN

SUSAN BONNINGTON was in a hurry as she drove her large black car down the winding lane leading to Hexwood Turkey Farm. She bounced up and down over the potholes and then braked hard as a tractor came out of a field ahead. She tooted the horn fiercely and then wound down her window. 'I say, you. Move!' she shouted.

Sam Woodyard turned to Carrot, sitting beside him on the tractor.

'Don't take no notice,' he said. 'It's her again.'

Behind them, Miss Bonnington hooted again. 'I'm in a hurry,' she shouted.

'Well I ain't,' muttered Sam and the two of them started to laugh.

The tractor continued to drive slowly down the lane and Miss Bonnington was forced to follow. 'Miss ruddy nuisance Bonnington,' said Sam to the accompaniment of the car hooter. 'I can't stand her.'

'Neither can I.'

'What's she want, anyway? She's always hangin' around.'

'She's coming to lunch,' said Carrot.

When the tractor finally reached the yard, the big car accelerated past them and drove up to the farmhouse. Carrot watched as his father came out to greet her.

'Beats me what Dad sees in her,' he said.

Sam grinned at him. 'Better get goin' old son, or you'll be late.'

Carrot took a deep breath as he went into the dining-room. Miss Bonnington was in full spate.

'Gave us a jolly good run. Viewed him across Gamley

Heath, drew Meddington Big Wood, and then we lost him. Daddy was livid.' She paused. 'Why don't you hunt, George?'

'I don't really have time, Susan,' said his father.

'Oh, hullo Edward,' said Miss Bonnington. 'Did you enjoy your joke?'

'What joke?' said Mr Bennet.

'I was forced to drive all the way down the lane behind the tractor,' she said. 'Thought it terribly funny, didn't you, Edward?'

'Go and get washed,' said Mr Bennet angrily, 'and put a clean shirt on.'

Lunch was misery. Carrot ate mechanically and watched them smiling at each other. Miss Bonnington kept making feeble jokes and his father laughed at them.

'I say,' she said suddenly, 'that boy's hair needs a jolly good cut!' Carrot glowered at her.

'You're right, so it does,' said his father.

'He'd better come with me this afternoon,' she laughed.

'When do you have to go?' asked Mr Bennet.

'Oh, my appointment's not till four.'

'That's splendid!'

'We've masses to talk about,' she smiled.

'Yes, we have,' replied Mr Bennet.

Carrot didn't like the way things were developing. He began to wonder if Catweazle could help him get rid of this woman; she was obviously after his father, and, unless she was stopped, she looked like getting him. He asked to be excused and got down from the table.

'Don't forget the hair, Edward,' said Miss Bonnington loudly.

'No,' he said, 'I won't.'

When he climbed into Castle Saburac, Catweazle was deep in a spell. Rapkyn's book lay open on a turkey box and the old man was scraping a long hazel stick with Adamcos, while Touchwood looked on phlegmatically.

'I will bind thee, Spirit of Time,' he muttered, 'By Meltraton, by Raziel, by Cassiel, and by . . . and by . . .' he referred to the book, ' 'tis so, by Azoth and Ysmael.'

He climbed on another box and drew an imaginary circle round himself with the hazel stick. 'Galbus, Galdat, Galdes, Galdat,' he intoned and then paused waiting for his spell to take effect, but with no result at all. 'Nothing works!' he said sadly.

He knelt by the box and twirled a twig against a piece of bark in an attempt to make fire.

'I didn't know you were in the Scouts,' said Carrot.

'Disturb me not, my brother, I make the Fire of Time.'

'I tried that once,' said Carrot. 'All you get is blisters.'

'Come no nearer!' said Catweazle as Carrot began to approach, 'Beware the Circle of Power,' and he pointed to the imaginary circle around him.

'Oh yes, of course,' said Carrot. 'All right if I cross my fingers?'

Catweazle nodded and then waved his arms in the air. 'Schempamporasch!' he exclaimed and beckoned to the boy. Carrot stepped carefully over the invisible circle with his fingers firmly crossed. 'What are you trying to do?' he asked.

'Return to my own time,' said Catweazle, who had already had enough of the twentieth century.

Carrot sighed. 'Catweazle, I wish you'd drop this daft idea about the past.'

Catweazle shook his head. When would the young sorcerer understand? He went back to his fire-making in silence, but it was a slow business.

'Here,' said Carrot after a while, 'have a match.'

Catweazle took the little stick with the tiny red bud

and examined it curiously, but Carrot had to light it for him.

'O Lucifer! O Morning Star!' cried Catweazle, falling backwards off the turkey box, 'truly thou art my master!' and he was so impressed that he completely forgot his spell.

Carrot, pleased with the effect that he had had, lit the fire with a flourish. Catweazle looked at him with envy. 'Great is thy power,' he said. 'Canst conjure fire at will?'

'Sure, it's easy,' he said, striking another match and blowing it out. 'You have a go,' and he handed the box to Catweazle. Carefully, the old man took out a match, and copying the boy, struck it. 'The Spirit whispers,' he said, watching with wonder as it burned. Carrot retrieved the box but Catweazle grabbed his arm. 'Give them to me,' he pleaded.

'No. I don't think I'd better.'

'But fire is power! Fire is a spirit! Give me the little sticks!'

'No,' said Carrot, 'you mustn't play with matches.'

'I beseech thee, master!'

Carrot looked at him. 'Tell you what,' he said, 'you can have the whole box, if you'll help me.'

'Verily, verily, O Prince of Fire!'

Carrot sat down and tried to explain about Miss Bonnington.

'That money we got for the head of Cernunnos doesn't seem to have made much difference. If Dad marries her, just to save the farm, life won't be worth living. You see, she's got pots of dough –'

'Pots of dough?' queried Catweazle.

'Anyway,' said Carrot, finding it hard to explain, 'I want to get rid of her, and I don't know how to do it.'

Catweazle sat twisting his beard round his finger. 'There are many ways to rid thyself of meddlers,' he said finally. 'Rapkyn will know.'

'She shall be blasted like a riven oak! Drowned in sulphur! Torn by whirlwinds!' he said as he turned the pages of the old book.

Carrot was a little taken aback. 'Couldn't we just scare her a bit?'

'Hear Rapkyn!' said Catweazle, finding the place. ' "To spite thine enemy: make thee a mannikin of wax, saying the while, be thou such an one. Burn garlic and vervain, and at the striking of the church bell at the seventh hour, take thou a long pin and pierce the image throughly." '

'Sounds a bit final, doesn't it?' said Carrot.

'Ay, it doth,' Catweazle grinned evilly. 'Hast thou wax?'

'Well, I've got some modelling clay. Look, Catweazle, don't you think we ought to think of something else?'

' "Provide thyself with any ring, thing or knick-knack of thine enemy's and tie it to thy doll," ' Catweazle read on remorselessly. Carrot was beginning to get worried.

'Any ring, thing or knick-knack?' he said. 'How are we going to get that?'

'Where is the woman?' asked Catweazle.

'She's still at the farm, but I can't just go and ask her, "Please Miss Bonnington can I have a ring, thing or knick-knack of yours, because I need it to put a spell on you!" '

'Thou art a dolt, brother in magic,' said Catweazle. 'We shall steal it from her.'

'Steal it!' Carrot was shocked, 'couldn't we just sort of borrow it and give it back afterwards?'

'Afterwards,' said Catweazle grimly, 'she may not need it!'

Carrot led the way back to the farm with considerable misgivings. The farm buildings gave them excellent cover and they managed to creep quite close to the house, where they hid behind some bags of fertilizer, only a few yards from the car.

Catweazle blew on his thumb-ring. 'Gab, gaba, agaba,' he said to the car.

'There might be something in the glove-compartment that would do,' whispered Carrot, and then ducked down as his father and Miss Bonnington came out of the house.

'I really will do my best, George,' she gushed.

'I'll have my fingers crossed,' said Mr Bennet, smiling as he opened the car door for her. Miss Bonnington put her handbag into the car and then stopped. 'Silly old me,' she said, 'I've forgotten the eggs!' Mr Bennet roared with laughter as if it was the funniest thing he had ever heard and the two of them went back into the house.

The car door was open and the handbag lay on the seat. Carrot felt terrible. He had never done anything like this before, but he had to save his father, so he ran over to the car and grabbed the bag. Catweazle followed and climbed over the seat to get a little red devil mascot that was hanging in the rear window. Carrot was still struggling to open the handbag when he heard Miss Bonnington and his father returning, so he threw it back on the seat and raced for cover.

'About nine I should think,' said Miss Bonnington as she reached the car, with her basket of eggs.

'I shall be waiting,' said his father.

Carrot was horrified. Catweazle was still in the car! He watched with dismay as it roared out of the yard, and, as his father went back into the house, he leapt on his bike and pursued Miss Bonnington up the lane.

The hairdresser's, Dorrice and Jayne, was at the far end of Westbourne High Street. Miss Bonnington's car was parked nearby and as Carrot cycled up, Catweazle's terrified face appeared at the window. He opened the door quickly and the old man fell out on to the pavement.

'Oh, oh!' he moaned, 'trees rushing past like storm clouds!'

'Did you get anything?'

'Nay, my brother! She was protected by Lucifer.' Catweazle held up the red devil mascot.

'So we can't use this as a thing or knick-knack?'

'Nay, 'tis a charm.'

Carrot led him over to the hairdresser's. 'She's in there,' he said. They looked in. The young receptionist sat at a small desk reading a magazine called *True Love*, and behind her, through a partition, several ladies draped in pink sat under the driers.

' 'Tis a torture chamber!' the magician said with horror.

'No it's not. It's a hairdresser's. They cut people's hair.'

'Monstrous! Monstrous!' muttered the sorcerer, 'Hair is magic, 'tis strength! Whoever hath thy hair hath power over thee!'

Carrot looked at him and then peered through the window to where Miss Bonnington sat having her hair trimmed. Small pieces of hair fell to the floor.

'You've given me an idea,' he said to Catweazle.

Inside Dorrice and Jayne's Miss Bonnington turned to the occupant of the next chair. 'You'll be at the meeting, Mrs Willoughby?' she asked coldly.

'I certainly will,' replied Mrs Willoughby, who was also having her hair trimmed.

'We can look forward to a long session then,' said Miss Bonnington, and then broke off in surprise when she saw Carrot at her elbow.

'Good heavens, Edward,' she said, 'I didn't really mean you to come!'

There was a sudden commotion from the receptionist's desk and a thin squeal of alarm. A moment later Catweazle rushed in through the partition and raised his arms above his head.

'Foolish wenches!' he yelled, dancing madly and waving his skinny arms. 'Three bitter bitter hath thee bitten,' he sang.

'He's dotty!' gasped Miss Bonnington.

'Three bitter bitter hath thee nippen!' Catweazle went on, capering like a demented Morris dancer.

'Phone for the police,' screamed an assistant, holding him at bay with her scissors.

'Three bitter bitter hath thee stricken!' sang Catweazle, prancing over to the driers where the ladies sat in a terrified row. Colliding with a trolley, he sat down on it, shot across the room and crashed into a giant vase full of paper flowers.

No one noticed Carrot scoop up a handful of hair as Catweazle rushed out into the street.

'Hey you, come back,' yelled Carrot running out after him. Round the corner they went to where Carrot's bike stood ready, and, with Catweazle perched precariously behind him, Carrot wobbled off downhill.

Later, Carrot was in the water tank helping to put the finishing touches to the doll.

'I do hope we're doing the right thing,' he said as they stuck on the hair.

'Ay, brother,' said Catweazle pointing to the spell in Rapkyn's book.

'I didn't mean that,' said Carrot. 'Oh well, never mind, we'll have to go through with it now, I suppose. Looks quite like her,' he added.

'It will serve,' said Catweazle, giving 'Miss Bonnington' a bit more chin.

'You're sure this new spell will be all right.'

'If that is thy wish.'

'Well I think it's better than piercing with a long pin.'

'Very well,' said Catweazle, disappointed, 'spots it shall be. Not boils?' he added hopefully.

'No, just spots. Lots of spots. All over. Like heat bumps,' explained Carrot.

'It shall be done.'

'Good! Now, don't forget what old Rapkyn says "At the striking of the church bell". Can you hear it from here?'

'Ay, brother, I have marked it. "At the seventh hour".'

He looked hopefully at Carrot, 'And the little fire sticks?'

Carrot took a match from the box. 'There you are,' he said. 'One on account, the rest if it works!'

But a shock awaited Carrot when he got back to the farm.

'Why don't you like Susan Bonnington?' said his father.

'I don't know, Dad,' said Carrot, feeling embarrassed.

'There must be a reason,' said Mr Bennet. Carrot glanced up at the cuckoo clock. It was nearly seven.

'Well, I just wish she didn't come here,' he said lamely.

'But why?' said Mr Bennet, puffing away at his pipe. 'You're so rude to her. You make it so obvious you don't like her.'

The clock struck seven. In Castle Saburac, Catweazle passed the doll backwards and forwards in the smoke of the burning garlic, and called down a plague of spots on Miss Bonnington.

'Ah!' said Mr Bennet glancing at the clock, 'the witching hour!'

'What did you say?' said Carrot horrified.

'The Council meets at seven you see. I hope she'll be able to swing it.'

'Swing what, Dad?' said Carrot.

'Well, I told you about the sheds I want to put up, and having to get the Council's permission didn't I? That's why I've been making such a fuss of Miss Bonnington. She's on the Council, you see.'

Carrot looked stunned. 'But I thought . . . that you and Miss Bonnington were going to – ' he stopped and Mr Bennet began to laugh.

'Oh Carrot, of course not. She's just trying to push my building plans through, that's all!'

'Oh crumbs!' said Carrot, 'oh crumbs!'

'Don't worry about it,' said his father. 'She'll be down later to tell us how it went. Those sheds would make a big difference to the farm.'

Carrot didn't know what to do. It was too late now anyway. The spell had been cast and Miss Bonnington was probably being driven to hospital in an ambulance at that very moment.

At ten o'clock Mr Bennet began to get worried. 'We should've heard from her by now,' he said.

'I don't think you're going to,' said Carrot miserably.

'Well that's a cheerful thing to say,' his father snapped.

Carrot decided to make a clean breast of it. 'Listen Dad,' he said, 'I know it's going to sound fantastic, but you'd better know the truth.' Before he could get any further, there was a ring at the door and Miss Bonnington burst into the room in triumph.

'George,' she said happily, 'you can start building next week.'

Carrot stared at her. She didn't have a single spot.

'Susan,' said his father, 'you're a brick. Isn't she Carrot?'

'Yes,' stammered the boy, still staring at her.

'What did you call him?' said Susan.

'Carrot.'

'That's nice,' she said. 'Suits him much better than Edward.'

'Was it a tough meeting?' said Mr Bennet, bringing her a drink.

'Would've been. Luckily my arch-enemy Mrs Willoughby was taken ill and had to go home. They think it's measles.'

'Measles!' said Carrot.

'Yes. Funny thing for a adult to catch. She seemed perfectly well in the hairdresser's this afternoon.'

Carrot could hardly wait to tell Catweazle how the spell had worked out. The two sorcerers sat side by side in Castle Saburac, their familiars on their laps, in front of the Sacred Fire.

Carrot handed over the matches in silence.

'Lucky I picked up the wrong hair. You really did make it work,' he said.

'Together, we did it together, my brother,' said Catweazle magnanimously. 'And Rapkyn's magic is very strong.'

'We must be careful next time, Catweazle. It could have been disaster.' Carrot held out his hand for the doll. 'I'd better have Miss Bonn – I mean Mrs Willoughby,' he corrected. 'Just in case you feel like having a practice.'

'Next time, hex time. From thy time to my time,' said Catweazle, making a magic sign.

'What d'you mean by that?' said Carrot, curiously.

The old man's eyes shone in the firelight, and, smiling his crooked smile, he struck another match with a flourish.

6

THE EYE OF TIME

CARROT and Catweazle sat fishing from an old punt in the middle of Kingfisher lake. It was a warm, still, summer morning. It had taken Carrot a long time to persuade Catweazle that it was safe in the punt, and now they sat, one at each end, watching the smooth black water for tell-tale bubbles.

Catweazle, fishing with a willow twig, a piece of string and a bent pin, occasionally sprang into action as he pulled another tench from the lake with expert ease. Carrot, however, had a shining new rod and had caught nothing.

'They're all up your end,' he muttered as Catweazle, giving a little chuckle, swung another fish on to the pile at his feet.

'I have done,' said the old sorcerer. ' 'Tis the thirteenth fish.'

'You mean it's unlucky?' said Carrot.

Catweazle snorted angrily. 'Always you mock me, brother in magic,' he said. 'Thou knowest full well, that for us of the Dark Path thirteen is great good luck. And the power of the Thirteenth Fish ...' He paused and tapped the side of his nose, 'well, thou knowest!'

Carrot, who had not the slightest idea what he was talking about, nodded wisely. 'Oh, yes, of course,' he said hurriedly. He opened a biscuit tin and passed Catweazle a sandwich.

Touchwood sat on the end of the punt catching flies and breathing heavily. Occasionally Catweazle splashed water over him to keep him cool.

'Luck's a funny thing,' said Carrot.

'Ay, 'tis most strange,' muttered Catweazle, crumbs falling from his beard.

'Sam's lucky, for instance. Well, sometimes. He bets on horses.'

'Bets on horses?'

Carrot sighed. He seemed to spend hours explaining things to Catweazle.

'You have to guess which horse will win a race,' he said slowly and carefully. 'They all get in a line, you see, and then they run towards a white post, and the first one past it is the winner. If you guessed the right horse you get some money.'

'Dost thou not know?' asked Catweazle with surprise.

'Know what?'

'The horses that will win.'

'Don't be silly,' said Carrot. 'How could you?'

Catweazle wondered if the young sorcerer was mocking him again.

'With the Eye of Time, brother, with the Eye of Time.'

'Oh, yes,' said Carrot, wondering what the Eye of Time was.

They paddled to the shore where Carrot had pitched his tent, and Catweazle lit a small fire, using his newly acquired matches. Then he placed the Thirteenth Fish on an improvised spit.

> 'From the water into the fire.
> From the fire into the earth,
> From the earth into the air'

sang Catweazle as he sprinkled marigold petals over the burning fish.

Suddenly, Carrot caught sight of his father's truck driving round the far side of the lake towards them.

'It's Dad!' he said, and pushed Catweazle into the tent.

Mr Bennet and Sam had been into Westbourne for supplies, and while his employer was busy ordering fertilizer, Sam had slipped away to visit Madame Rosa, the local fortune-teller. He often went to see her to ask for the names of horses that were going to win. She would gaze into her crystal ball, pretending to see into the future, while she read out names from a racing paper hidden under the table on her lap. Then Sam would go next door to the betting shop and place his bets. What he didn't know was that the betting shop was run by Madame Rosa's husband; working together, they were running a very profitable business.

Unfortunately Mr Bennet had caught Sam before he had managed to place his bets and had made him get into the truck.

'But I ain't bin in yet!' Sam had protested.

'Then I've saved you some money,' Mr Bennet had replied.

Now, as the two men walked up to the tent, Carrot signalled to Catweazle to keep very quiet.

'Any luck?' said Mr Bennet.

'Yes,' said Carrot, 'I've caught a lot.'

'I told you, you needed a decent rod. We're going to measure the ground for the new sheds. You'll make sure that fire's out before you go, won't you, Carrot?' said his father turning back to the truck.

Sam waited until Mr Bennet was out of earshot and then he spoke.

'You going back to the farm afore this afternoon?'

'Why?' said Carrot. 'Do you want me to put some bets on for you?'

'How did you know?' asked Sam, getting a piece of paper from his pocket.

'Because it's Saturday,' said Carrot taking the paper.

'Better make it five bob each way,' grinned Sam.

As Carrot wrote this down, Catweazle watched suspiciously from the tent. What plot was the young sorcerer hatching?

'Come on, Sam!' Mr Bennet called from the truck.

'Comin' Mr Bennet,' called Sam. He turned back to Carrot. 'You'll get them on in time, won't you?'

'Of course I will.'

'An' if they come up, there'll be a couple of bob for you,' said Sam as he began to run back to the truck.

Carrot waved as it drove off and then Catweazle emerged from the tent and glowered at him.

'What spell didst thou write?' he asked.

'It's not a spell, it's Sam's bets for this afternoon.'

'Ah! The horses that will win,' said Catweazle.

'If he's lucky.'

'Hath he the Eye of Time?'

'I don't know. What is it?'

Catweazle held out his wrinkled hand. 'Give me thy paper,' he said. Carrot handed it over and Catweazle sat down crosslegged while the smoke from the fire rose into the air.

'Where do these swift horses run?' he asked.

'Lingfield and Newmarket,' said Carrot.

Catweazle held the bit of paper against his forehead and closed his eyes. Carrot looked at him anxiously.

'Have you got a headache?'

'Peace brother.'

'Sorry.'

Catweazle began to sway backwards and forwards.

'O Spirits of the Brazen Vessel, I call on thee,' he intoned. 'Sator, Arepo, Tenet, Opera, Rotas!'

He stopped swaying and the piece of paper fluttered down. His eyes opened but they saw nothing.

'Lingfield,' he whispered, 'Lingfield! A multitude roaring like the sea! Men wave their arms. Spells are spoken. The horses thunder past a white post. A bird flying through the rain. The moon turns blue over the mighty oak. The shouting dies away. 'Tis done, 'tis done.'

Slowly Catweazle's eyes lost their blind stare and he turned to Carrot and scratched himself. The wood crackled on the fire.

'Well?' said Carrot eagerly, 'who's going to win?'

'Ass-eared turnspit!' said Catweazle rising impatiently.

'But I thought you were going to tell me the winners!'

'Thou art a fool! The Eye of Time is shut to thee! I go to Castle Saburac, and better company!' And picking up Touchwood Catweazle strode off angrily into the wood.

Carrot was still puzzling why he had been so angry when he got back to the farm. Then he remembered Sam's bets and phoned the betting shop, stuffing a handkerchief in his mouth to disguise his voice.

'Sam Woodyard here,' he mumbled through the handkerchief, giving the account number. He had often helped like this when Sam hadn't been able to get to the phone himself.

'Yes, Mr Woodyard?' said the bookie.

'Lingfield. Two thirty, Kettledrum; three fifteen, Royal Court,' said Carrot, reading from Sam's piece of paper.

'Got that,' said the bookie. 'You got a shocking cold, mate.'

'Newmarket,' Carrot went on, 'four o'clock, Black Beauty. And they're all five bob each way.'

Later, when Sam was working in one of the fattening sheds, Carrot, who had watched the race on television, came in with the result of the two-thirty.

'Well?' said Sam, 'did Kettledrum win?'

'No,' said Carrot, 'it was a horse called Rainbird.'

'Rainbird!' Sam was disgusted. 'That's the last time I go to Madame Rosa!'

'Gosh!' said Carrot suddenly, ' "a bird flying through the rain." '

'What's that old son?'

Carrot sat down on a bale of straw. 'A bird flying through the rain', Catweazle had said, and the winning horse had been Rainbird. What else had the old man said? Something about the moon and a tree. 'The moon turns blue, over the mighty oak.' Yes, that was it!

'Are you all right, Carrot?' Sam asked anxiously, seeing his rather dazed expression.

'Is there a horse called Mighty Oak running this afternoon?' asked Carrot.

'Yes,' said Sam, 'in the four o'clock at Newmarket.'

Carrot gasped. 'What about Blue Moon?' he said.

'Blue Moon's in the three-fifteen at Lingfield. What's all this about, Carrot? Has someone given you a tip?'

It was true then, thought Carrot. Catweazle could pick the winners. That was what he meant by the Eye of Time!

'Listen, Sam,' he said, 'we've got to change those bets of yours. Blue Moon and Mighty Oak are going to win.'

'But I've backed Royal Court and Black Beauty.'

'I don't care! They haven't a chance! I just know it!'

'Take it easy, Carrot,' said Sam, 'them bets is laid now an' I don't want 'em changed.'

'All right,' said Carrot. 'But don't say I didn't tell you.'

In his bedroom, Carrot emptied out his money box. There was about three pounds in bits and pieces. The model aeroplane would have to wait, he thought. Anyhow, with Catweazle to tell him the winners, he would make a fortune. He would be able to buy his father the grain drier he wanted, and Sam could have a sports car. He glanced at his watch. Only half an hour to get Catweazle to the betting shop.

Carrot ran all the way to the water tower.

'Catweazle!' he gasped as he stumbled down into the tank, 'I'm sorry. I didn't understand. But I do now, and I think you're the greatest magician in the world.'

Catweazle was very surprised to see the young sorcerer so humble.

'So, thou jackdaw, thou singest a new song now!'

'You've got to come with me, into Westbourne,' said Carrot urgently.

'Nay,' said Catweazle, 'I fear the enchanted chariots.'

'But we're brothers, remember?'

'Mayhap, mayhap,' said Catweazle deliberately keeping Carrot on tenterhooks.

'Please, Catweazle! It's a special magic and I can't do it without you. I haven't got the Eye of Time, you see.'

Catweazle took a little longer to decide before the two of them finally set off across the fields to Westbourne. They passed a scarecrow and Carrot took off its hat and coat and gave them to Catweazle.

'Better stick these on,' he said. 'You won't look quite so . . . er . . . conspicuous.'

Catweazle was very against wearing anything other than his robe, but Carrot insisted. 'We'll pick up your robe on the way back!' he said as he pushed the unwilling magician into the old mac. With his long hair sticking out round the hat, and rabbit-skin boots under the mac, Catweazle looked very odd indeed.

'I am no longer Catweazle,' he complained.

'That's the idea,' said Carrot.

They continued across the fields until they came to Westbourne. The town frightened Catweazle and he kept close to Carrot. Outside the betting shop stood a small group of men, chatting and reading the papers.

'Stay here,' said Carrot, 'I won't be a moment,' and he went into the shop.

A loudspeaker was blaring as Carrot approached the counter, and a red faced man with his shirt sleeves rolled up and a pencil behind each ear looked up at him.

'Hop it,' he said.

'But listen,' said Carrot.

'Can't you read?' said the man, pointing to a large notice.

'No person under eighteen is allowed on these premises,' read Carrot.

'That's right,' said the man, 'so hop it.'

'Look,' said Carrot, 'I've got a foreign friend outside and he doesn't speak much English.'

'Is he over eighteen?'

'Oh, yes,' said Carrot. 'Well over.'

'O.K.' said the man. 'Write down what he wants outside and then send him in with it. And the money,' he added.

But when Carrot looked outside Catweazle had vanished and the farm truck was parked by the betting shop with his father inside.

'Come here,' said Mr Bennet grimly.

'Listen Dad – '

'Get in.'

They drove off in silence. Carrot looked at his father's angry face, and finally plucked up courage to speak.

'I wanted to help the farm – ' he began.

'By hanging around betting shops?' interrupted his father angrily.

There was a pause.

'Did Sam tell you?' asked Carrot.

'I found this by the television,' said his father. It was Sam's list with 'five bob each way' scribbled underneath in Carrot's handwriting.

'I tackled Sam about it,' said Mr Bennet, 'and he told me the whole story. I'm prepared to forget it Carrot, if you promise never to try anything like this again. Sam has already promised he won't ask you.'

'I promise, Dad,' said Carrot. 'And thanks.'

'Good!' Mr Bennet relaxed and smiled at his son. 'If you really want to help the farm you can't beat hard work, you know.'

Carrot, who had expected a worse punishment from his father, sat back and began to wonder what had happened to Catweazle.

While Carrot had been in the betting shop, Catweazle had recognized the signs of the Zodiac on Madame

Rosa's notice next door, and, following the pointing arrow, he had climbed the stairs to the fortune-teller's waiting-room. Perhaps this magician was the one who could help him return to his own time.

'Yes, dear?' said Madame Rosa peering through a bead curtain. She was a large woman and she wore a black shiny dress. On her head was an ornate turban, and large gold earrings jingled from her ears.

'Horse and Hattock,' said Catweazle. It was an ancient password used by witches. 'Hast thou the Eye of Time?'

Madame Rosa, who was a little bit deaf, glanced at her watch. 'Yes dear,' she said. 'It's ten past three. If you want a sitting, that will be seven-and-six.'

'Seven-and-six,' muttered Catweazle, adding them together to make thirteen. ' 'Tis good!'

Pushing his way through the curtain, he looked at the witch's room. There were velvet hangings, embroidered with writhing dragons, and the whole place was crammed with ornate Chinese carvings. In the midst of all this oriental splendour, three plaster ducks flew up the dark red wallpaper. It all looked rather inviting to Catweazle.

The object that he found most fascinating was a large crystal ball standing in the middle of the table.

'Ah!' he said. ' 'Tis a giant scrying glass! Like a full moon! I feel its power!' and he stretched out his hands over it as if warming them.

'Oh, you mean my crystal?' said Madame Rosa nervously. 'I don't know what I'd do without that. Some people use tea-leaves, you know, but it's such a messy business. I always think the ball is more artistic. Do sit down.'

'Six to four the field!' squawked a scruffy looking parrot from a cage in the corner of the room.

Catweazle looked at the bird in amazement, and crossed his fingers.

'Art thou a Spirit?'

The parrot eyed him maliciously. 'They're off! They're off!' it cried.

'Now, now, Laura. There's a good girl,' soothed Madame Rosa. 'I've had her for years,' she said to Catweazle. 'I've got goldfish for tranquillity, but it's not the same as someone talking to you, is it?'

She took a chocolate from a box on the table. 'Shouldn't eat these in front of her. She gets very jealous, and they're not good for her.'

' 'Tis a Demon!' said Catweazle.

'Well, she can be a bit of a demon at times, but she's a heart of gold, haven't you my angel?' she said to the parrot. The bird glared at her malevolently and picked up a nut in its claw. 'Shut up Laura!' it screeched in a passable imitation of Madame Rosa.

'And now to work, as they say,' said the fortune-teller sitting down opposite Catweazle.

'May I hold a personal possession of yours? It helps the vibrations. Any familiar object.'

'Familiar?' said Catweazle, 'ay!' and he put Touchwood into her outstretched hand.

'Aaaaaah!' screamed Madame Rosa, jumping up and dropping the toad on the table. Touchwood crawled up to the crystal ball and gazed at himself in the glass.

'Take it away! Ugh! The nasty slimy thing!'

Catweazle put Touchwood back in his pocket, puzzled by the witch's behaviour.

'Why do you carry a dreadful thing like that around with you?' she said.

'I am a magician,' said Catweazle with great dignity.

'Oh, I see! A magician! Oh, I get quite a lot of theatrical people in, you know. There's a ventriloquist who comes every fortnight.' She took another chocolate from the box. 'What do you call yourself?' she asked.

'Catweazle.'

'How very unusual. Are you appearing anywhere at the moment?' she asked.

'Ay,' said Catweazle sadly. 'Here.'

'Yes, well, shall we look into the crystal?' she said, crouching over the table. Catweazle also peered into the ball and, as their heads bumped, they looked at each other, nose to nose, over the top.

'What are you doing?' Madame Rosa asked irritably.

'Looking,' said Catweazle.

'You don't do it, I do it,' she said. 'I see a long journey, you will travel far.'

'Ay, 'tis true.'

'You're a very lucky person, did you know? You ought to have a little flutter now and then.'

Catweazle glanced at the parrot. A little flutter? Was the witch going to turn him into a bird? He crossed his fingers and blew on his thumb-ring.

'Dost seek to enchant me?' he said, rising from the table.

'What on earth's the matter with you? I only suggested – '

'Thou canst not gain power over me.' He looked at her, suddenly realizing she was a sham. ' 'Tis all pretence.'

'What did you say?'

' 'Tis all pretence,' said Catweazle getting excited. 'Thine eye is shut. Thou knowest nothing!'

'I've never been so insulted,' said Madame Rosa, also getting to her feet, and putting the chocolates safely behind her on the chair. 'You get out of here, Mr Catferret, or whatever your name is – '

'Cease thy squalling, thou shrew!' shouted Catweazle at the top of his voice. 'I see all clearly, like a hovering hawk. Thy name is Ethel, thy man's name is Albert. Many men give him gold for the horses. Thou sendest them to him, saying that they will have good fortune.'

Madame Rosa stared at Catweazle. 'How did you find out?'

'Mine eye is open. I have the Eye of Time,' and before the amazed fortune-teller could stop him Catweazle grabbed the crystal ball.

'Put that down!' she cried, fighting for possession.

'They're off! They're off!' screamed the parrot. 'Six to four the field.' Suddenly Madame Rosa lost her hold on the crystal ball and sat down on the box of chocolates. With a cry of glee Catweazle hugged it to him and vanished down the stairs while Madame Rosa collapsed in hysterics.

7

THE ENCHANTING BOX

In the strange half light before dawn Catweazle sat in Castle Saburac hunched over his new scrying glass. The candles were lit and the Sacred Fire was burning. Beside him, on one of the boxes, Touchwood squatted, puffing himself out complacently.

The magician, once more wearing his ragged robe, stared intently into the crystal ball.

'See, Touchwood,' he muttered. 'In the scrying glass, the years melting like snow.' He paused and threw some ivy leaves into the fire.

'I have eaten mugwort,' he told his familiar. 'Soon I shall see down the well of time; our past lies there.' He bent closer. 'The glass is clearing. The clouds roll away. I see the trees of the forest. Look there, look there!'

As the sun came up he made the invocation to the Spirits of the Brazen Vessel, reading carefully from Rapkyn's book. It was true that the book was from a later time than his own, but he felt sure that with its help he would return to the past. With nothing more to do until sunset, when he had to begin the Great Spell, Catweazle went off to search for food.

He was a first-class scavenger. In his own time he had often gone foraging at night, creeping silently from the forest and taking whatever he could find from lonely Saxon farmsteads. It had become part of his nature to collect things.

His search led him to the edge of the wood, where he found a ruined cottage. It had been empty for many years and part of the roof had collapsed. The windows were all broken and the door hung crazily from its hinges.

Catweazle looked at it for several minutes and then sniffing suspiciously, he approached it, blowing on his magic thumb-ring. 'Gab, gaba, agaba,' he muttered as he crept inside.

The place was a treasure house! On the floor was a large pile of rubbish. Eagerly the sorcerer began to hunt through rusty tin cans, old bedsprings and broken pieces of china. Everything bewildered him and at the same time he was enchanted by it.

'See, Touchwood!' cried Catweazle, holding up an old roller skate. ' 'Tis a chariot for thee!'

Touchwood's throat pulsed quickly as Catweazle put him on the roller skate. For a moment he endured the rusty iron against his belly and then he flopped off on to the floor again, and crawled away in search of beetles while his master went on picking over the pile of rubbish.

He found many things, but none that he recognized. There was an old aluminium coffee pot, a hockey stick, a bicycle pump and an old electric iron. He placed these mysterious objects around him and sat on the floor.

While he was trying to puzzle out what they were for, Carrot's head suddenly appeared round the door.

'So that's where you got to,' he said. 'I've been looking all over for you.'

'And thou hast found me,' said Catweazle calmly.

'Well, you can't stay here,' said Carrot, pulling Catweazle to his feet. 'Dad's on his way up. He's bringing someone to look at this place. It's for sale you see.'

'Let me be, thou cobweb!' snapped Catweazle.

'What are you doing here anyway?' asked Carrot.

Catweazle pointed proudly to the rusty things on the floor. 'See the treasures I have gleaned,' he said, beginning to put them into an old sack. An old boot followed the other rubbish as he continued to rummage through the junk. Then he picked up a battered suitcase.

'What is this?' he asked.

'A suitcase,' replied Carrot. 'You know, for travelling.'

'For travelling?' said Catweazle softly. 'Then I will take it.'

This last remark was lost on Carrot who had just seen his father and the two American ladies who wanted to look at the cottage.

'They're here!' he said, making for the back door. Catweazle took one quick look out of the window and made off after Carrot with his sack and his suitcase.

'It's just great,' said Eleanor Derringer looking at the cottage. The famous photographer clicked the shutter of her expensive Japanese camera and then glanced up in surprise.

'Oh!' she said, turning to Mr Bennet and her companion, 'did you see him?'

'See who?' said Mr Bennet.

'There's someone in there,' she said, pointing towards the cottage.

'I'll take a look. Probably a tramp,' said Mr Bennet.

As he went to the front door, Carrot and Catweazle ran out of the back.

'Did they see you?' whispered Carrot as the two of them hid in the long grass but Catweazle shook his head. They waited and saw Mr Bennet go back to Mrs Derringer.

'I guess that hobo got a shock,' she said. 'Didn't you see him, Maud?' Maud, a thin, pale, long-suffering woman with most of Mrs Derringer's photographic equipment hanging from her, shook her head. 'No Eleanor,' she said.

'The place has been empty for years,' said Mr Bennet. 'So tramps tend to move in. They're an awful nuisance. It's one of the reasons I want to do the place up.'

'I think it's perfect! I want to buy it,' said Mrs Derringer.

'You'll have to spend a lot of money,' said Mr Bennet. 'It hasn't got electricity.'

'I don't care. I'm buying peace and tranquillity, and a little bit of England,' said the photographer, and she went into the cottage with the others.

'People!' snorted Catweazle, getting to his feet.

'What's wrong with people?' said Carrot, carrying the sack for him as they moved away.

'They make my head buzz.'

'That's because you're not used to them.'

'No, and do not want to be.'

Carrot stopped. 'You're used to me though, aren't you?'

Catweazle didn't answer.

'So what do you think of me?'

'Think of you?' said Catweazle, looking puzzled. 'But you are here.'

'But when I'm not here?' asked Carrot.

'Then I do not think of you,' said Catweazle.

There was a long silence as they walked along, the sack clanking on Carrot's back.

'It's not good to be alone,' he said. 'You're alone too much.'

'I lived alone in my own time.'

'This is your own time,' said Carrot, getting angry. 'Can't you see? Here and now!'

Catweazle looked at the boy's face and slowly shook his head.

'Here and now I am,' he said. 'There and then, I want to be.'

'But it's a dream, Catweazle.'

'Nettleface!' said Catweazle, gesturing round him. 'This is the dream.'

They arrived at the base of the water tower and he took the sack from Carrot.

'Leave me,' he said.

'But I'll help you up with them,' said Carrot.

'Nay,' said the old magician.

'What's the matter? Why can't I come up?'

'There is a circle of power round Saburac,' said Catweazle looking up at the rusty water tank.

'What for? You're being very mysterious. Is it another spell?'

'All is prepared. Farewell, brother.'

'I don't know what's got into you today,' said Carrot. 'I'll see you later.'

Catweazle watched until the boy was out of sight and then he shook his head. 'See me later?' he muttered.

A new batch of two thousand chicks had arrived when Carrot got back to the farm and Sam was busily supervising their unloading. Mr Bennet returned from showing Mrs Derringer the way back to Tollington Hall, where she and Maud were staying, and everybody worked hard to get the chicks safely into the brooders.

During the afternoon, while Sam and Carrot were busy cleaning out one of the sheds, they heard a car coming down the lane.

'Hear that?' said Sam excitedly. 'That's a Merc!'

With a final throbbing roar and a squeak from the brakes a beautiful snow-white sports car pulled up in the yard. The strange gobbling cry rose from the turkey pens.

'It's Edward, isn't it?' said Mrs Derringer as she and her assistant climbed out. 'We've come to see your Pa again. About the cottage.'

'Isn't this super!' said Carrot admiring the car.

'With some women it's hats but with me it's sports cars,' said Mrs Derringer complacently.

Maud pursed her lips and said nothing.

'Oh, by the way, Edward,' said Mrs Derringer, getting a photo from the glove compartment, 'have you ever seen this man before?'

Carrot gasped. It was an enlargement of Catweazle caught peering through the window of the ruined cottage.

'Something wrong?' said Mrs Derringer.

'Er, no,' said Carrot.

'I took him this morning when I photographed the cottage. I said I'd seen him, didn't I Maud? So I developed the picture and there he was.'

Sam went by, pausing to admire the car, so Carrot quickly held the enlargement to his chest.

'Do you know him?' asked Mrs Derringer, who had not been a reporter for nothing.

'Well, yes, sort of,' said Carrot, breathing a sigh of relief as Sam went back to his work.

'Who is he?' said Mrs Derringer.

'I don't really know,' said Carrot. 'He's a sort of hermit.'

'Lovely! D'you think he would pose?'

'Pose?'

'I want to take pictures of him for my new book.'

'Oh, I don't think he'd like that very much,' said Carrot hastily.

Mr Bennet came out of the farmhouse and waved to the two ladies. Mrs Derringer smiled her wide American smile. 'See if you can find him for me,' she said and left Carrot gaping at the enlargement in his hand. After all he'd done to keep Catweazle hidden! 'I must warn him,' thought Carrot and ran off through the farmyard.

When he reached Castle Saburac he gave his usual whistle and then hurriedly climbed the ladder. As he reached the top Catweazle's head appeared through the inspection hole.

'You will spoil all. All!' he said angrily.

'So will you,' said Carrot. 'Look at this!' He held up the picture. Catweazle uttered a terrible cry and disappeared down the hole. There was a crash.

'Jolly well serves you right,' said Carrot climbing into the tank.

'Schempamporasch!' shouted the sorcerer, waving his hazel wand frantically. 'Nothing works!' he moaned as Carrot ignored the magic command and came nearer.

Carrot was bewildered by the old man's terror.

'I will obey thee, master! I will obey!'

'What?'

'Do not pretend with me,' said Catweazle. 'My being is in thy power. Thou hast my image, thou treacherous cunning fox!'

'What are you talking about?'

'See, I am in thy hands,' said Catweazle pointing to the photograph.

Carrot paused. 'You mean whoever's got a picture of you can make you do anything that they want?'

'Mock me not! Thou knowest 'tis so.'

Carrot shrugged and handed the photograph to Catweazle who took it with amazed relief and tore it into tiny pieces.

'Now I am safe,' he muttered.

'But I didn't take that picture,' said Carrot with dismay, 'Mrs Derringer took it and she'll be furious!'

'Without the Magic Face the hag hath no power over me.'

'Don't be daft,' said Carrot. 'She's got the negative. She can make as many copies as she likes.'

This remark had a disastrous effect on Catweazle. His arms fell to his sides and he looked utterly defeated.

'If my image is with her, I am her slave.'

'No you're not, she's only a photographer.'

'I must find her,' said Catweazle dully. And, as if he was walking in his sleep, he climbed out of Castle Saburac.

Nothing that Carrot could say seemed to have any effect. Catweazle marched through the wood looking straight ahead. He might have been deaf.

'You can't go!' said Carrot. 'Anything might happen to you.'

When they reached the road, Catweazle stopped and looked towards the farm.

'She comes,' he muttered tonelessly. 'I hear her chariot.' He stood motionless and apathetic, waiting until the shining car drove up to them.

'Why, hello there!' said Mrs Derringer, smiling at Catweazle while Maud looked on disapprovingly. 'You got my message?'

'I am yours,' said Catweazle, totally resigned.

'Oh, how charming,' said Mrs Derringer. 'And so clever of Edward to find you.'

'Oh, that's all right,' said Carrot miserably, feeling that matters were now out of his hands.

'Climb aboard,' Mrs Derringer said to Catweazle. 'You'll have to perch in the back, O.K.?'

Catweazle scrambled on to the car and lay across it like a condemned man at an execution. Mrs Derringer waved at Carrot and off they went.

For Catweazle, the journey seemed like unending torture. The car tore down the twisting country roads with Mrs Derringer driving dangerously fast. The magician held on as best he could, with his eyes tightly closed. His long white hair blew about and his teeth chattered with fear. The car swayed round the bends and almost took off over the hump-backed bridges.

As Mrs Derringer drove up to Tollington Hall, he finally opened his eyes.

'Here we are,' she said.

Catweazle slid off the back of the car and sat down heavily in the drive.

'Guess you're not used to fast cars,' said Mrs Derringer.

'I think he's going to be sick,' said Maud.

'Nonsense, Maud!' said Mrs. Derringer, helping him to his feet and leading him indoors like a sacrifice.

He was made to sit on a high stool while the witch moved towards him and then away again in a strange ritual. Grinning evilly at him, she twisted her body into ungainly positions and bent over a silver box from which grew a hideous round black eye. She kept blinding him with her magic. Lightning flashed, but there was no thunder.

When the photographic session was over, Mrs Derringer and Maud disappeared into the improvised dark-room, leaving Catweazle trembling and shaken. What potions were the witches brewing, he thought? What spells? What enchantments?

It was some time later that the photographer and her assistant returned to find him in exactly the same position still frozen with fear. Mrs Derringer pinned half a dozen assorted Catweazles, wet from the fixing tank, to a large screen, while Maud made the tea.

'There,' said Mrs Derringer. 'I really think I've caught you, don't you?'

Catweazle looked at the pictures. 'Ay,' he said.

'You know,' she said, trying to put him at his ease, 'I haven't even asked you your name yet. What is it?'

'Catweazle,' he said unhappily.

'Oh, really! Just Catweazle?'

Maud arrived with the tea-trolley and Mrs Derringer gave Catweazle a large piece of cake. After sniffing it and deciding that it wasn't enchanted, he had an exploratory chew. Maud sniffed her disapproval.

'Command me! I am your slave!' said Catweazle suddenly.

Mrs Derringer whispered to Maud. 'I think he wants to work here.

'You're crazy if you trust him,' whispered Maud.

'Why ever not? If he really wants to help.'

'I am your slave!' Catweazle repeated, standing up. 'I will obey.'

'You make me feel like Aladdin,' giggled Mrs Derringer. 'If you really want to help, I'm sure we can find something for you to do.'

When Carrot cycled up to Tollington Hall to see what had happened to Catweazle, he found him standing by the white sports car holding a bucket of water in one hand and a car washing mop in the other. Before he could stop him, Catweazle lifted the bucket and emptied it into the front seats.

'What on earth d'you think you're doing?' said Carrot.

'Save thyself, brother. She hath the enchanting box,' said Catweazle, pointing to the garden where the two ladies were sunning themselves.

'Catweazle, you've got to pull yourself together.'

'I cannot. The hag hath torn me apart, into many parts.'

'But just because you've been photographed it doesn't mean she owns you.'

'Fly, brother,' said Catweazle, dully, 'while there is still time.'

'Listen to me,' said Carrot. 'If I get those pictures, will you come back to Castle Saburac?'

'I know not,' said Catweazle listlessly.

'You're useless!' said Carrot angrily. 'If they start to come back – press this,' he said, pointing to the horn button on the steering wheel, and he crept into the house.

Catweazle stared at the button. What would happen if he did press this thing? Would Demons come to his aid? Or might he become invisible? The temptation was too much for him. Slowly his finger approached the button and finally jabbed at it. It stuck. The horn blared out, and Catweazle shook with terror.

Carrot, who was reaching for the last picture in the sitting-room, jumped back in alarm and the screen came crashing down on the tea trolley. Cups broke and the teapot rolled over the carpet as he rushed out.

'You idiot!' he shouted at Catweazle above the nerve-shattering noise of the horn. 'Here! You're free! Now get going!'

As Catweazle grabbed the pictures, he suddenly came to life. His eyes lit up again and he made off like a hare down the drive, leaving Carrot to prise up the horn button with his penknife.

'Edward, what are you doing?' said Mrs Derringer as she came running up with Maud.

'The horn was jammed,' said Carrot.

'Where's Mr Catweazle?'

'Gone.'

Maud glanced significantly at Mrs Derringer and ran indoors.

'Where did he go?' said Mrs Derringer.

'I don't know,' said Carrot. 'He didn't say.'

There was a scream from the sitting-room and Maud came running out again.

'He's smashed the place up and taken the prints! He must be mad!' she said excitedly.

'Then let's get after him!' said Mrs Derringer.

They jumped in the car and sat down on the wet seats. A shocked expression appeared on their faces as the water soaked through. Then the powerful car burst into life with a roar and skidded off in pursuit of their prey.

Catweazle ran panting into the woods, tearing the photos into little pieces and scattering them behind him like confetti.

'Hag ridden, thou midden,' he gasped, reciting a spell. 'Hag turnabout, thus I thee rout.' He waved his arms in the air. 'Schempamporasch,' he cried.

Was it Catweazle's magic or merely coincidence that at that moment a front tyre burst on Mrs Derringer's car and she was forced to abandon the chase?

Catweazle ran on until he reached the water tower. The sun was beginning to set.

'Always I am hunted, used and abused,' he said. 'Now all is sorcery, magic I cannot learn, magic I cannot vanquish. I will return to the past and the mighty forest. 'Tis time to make the Great Spell.'

He climbed into the tank, and made his final preparations. Putting the junk from the cottage into the suitcase together with the crystal ball he placed it in the centre of his magic circle and lit the candles with Carrot's matches.

'*Venite spiritus, coeli et terrae, ignis et aquae, ab hoc loco abripite me,*' commanded Catweazle.

Carrot, who had seen Catweazle making for the water tower, began to climb up himself.

'Asparaspes!' shouted Catweazle. 'Askoraskis!'

He looked around. He was still in the water tank.

'Salmay, Dalmay, Adonay!' he cried, as Carrot reached the top of the ladder outside and began to climb in.

'That was a near thing,' said Carrot. He stopped in bewilderment. In the magic circle stood the suitcase of rubbish and Rapkyn's book lay open on a turkey box with the hazel wand propped against it, but of Touchwood and Catweazle there was no sign. They had disappeared.

8

THE TELLING BONE

THE next morning Ted Wilkins, the verger of St Edmunds, Banden, looked up at the church steeple and saw a man clinging to it about two feet below the weather cock.

He shaded his eyes and peered up at the man.

'What are you up to?' he called.

Catweazle, who had spent a miserable night wondering where he was, looked down at the figure in the churchyard and shook with fright.

'Nothing works!' he groaned.

Wilkins, convinced that the whole thing was a practical joke, probably aimed at him, walked slowly over to the vicarage, where he found the vicar, a big smooth-faced man, knocking croquet-hoops into the lawn.

'There's a feller on the spire,' said Wilkins laconically.

'What's that, Wilkins?' said the vicar.

'On the spire,' Wilkins repeated patiently. 'There's this feller.'

The vicar put down his mallet. What was the man babbling about?

'Better come,' said Wilkins darkly. 'In case he falls.'

The sight of Catweazle hanging on to the spire had already attracted a small group of onlookers. The vicar pushed his way through them.

'Stand back!' he commanded. 'He may be going to jump!'

The group scattered hurriedly.

'He ain't going to jump,' said Wilkins cynically. 'It's a publicity stunt if you ask me. Next thing one of these hellycopters will come over and start chuckin' down packets of cornflakes.'

'Get a ladder,' ordered the vicar, ignoring Wilkins's flight of fancy. 'I am going up to the belfry.'

'I'll get the police,' said Wilkins.

'No,' said the vicar. 'He's on my spire and I shall deal with him. The poor man's obviously demented.'

'Don't do anything foolish!' he shouted up to Catweazle. 'We must talk this thing over. Whatever you do, don't jump!'

Catweazle, who had no intention of jumping, gripped the spire desperately. Touchwood poked his head out of his pocket, but, after a quick look, stuck it back in again. Eventually the vicar, helped by Wilkins, managed to get a ladder through the trapdoor of the belfry and lean it against the spire.

While Wilkins supported the base, the vicar, hampered a bit by his long black cassock, climbed shakily up towards Catweazle.

'Is it trouble with the police?' he asked.

There was no reply.

'Financial difficulties?'

Again there was no reply.

'I mean,' said the vicar, adopting his best professional manner, 'whatever the problem is, it can be solved. Helping people is my job, you know.'

The ladder wobbled. In a sudden panic, the vicar looked down at Wilkins. 'Hold it still, you fool,' he yelled.

'You'll never shift him, Vicar,' said Wilkins. 'He's made up his mind to be awkward.'

'Salmay, Dalmay, Adonay!' cried Catweazle. 'Let me fly!'

'Oh, I really would advise against any attempt to fly,' the vicar said hurriedly.

'*Venite, venite spiritus!*' called Catweazle, hoping that the Spirits of the Brazen Vessel might help.

Hearing the Latin, the vicar took heart. The man was obviously educated: no doubt fallen on hard times.

'*Dum vivimus, vivamus,*' he said cheerfully. 'Where there's life, there's hope. If you come down to, er, *terra firma* things might look very different. I mean, *nil desperandum*, old chap!'

Catweazle looked at the big man in the long black robe with interest. Clearly he was a fellow sorcerer.

'Dost thou follow the Path?' he muttered, uneasily.

'Well, I try, you know, I try. Narrow though it is,' said the vicar.

'I have failed,' said Catweazle. The Great Spell had gone very wrong.

'We all do. But sometimes it's a blessing in disguise.'

'Art thou my brother?' asked Catweazle, showing the vicar his magic thumb-ring.

The vicar, mistaking the meaning of Catweazle's gesture, clasped him by the hand. 'Of course! Of course!'

'Then thou wilt show me thy book?' Perhaps this sorcerer had better spells than Rapkyn's, thought Catweazle.

'Gladly,' said the vicar, feeling he was making real progress. 'I'll give you a copy.'

'Then I will descend,' said Catweazle.

'Thank heavens for that!' said the vicar, who really had no head for heights.

Catweazle slithered down the spire, nearly knocking the vicar off the ladder, and then slowly made his way down, through the belfry.

The vicar took Catweazle across the churchyard and ushered him into his study at the vicarage. It was a typical bachelor's study, comfortable and old fashioned, with squashy armchairs and an old desk piled high with papers. There was a white telephone, a set of golf clubs, and books piled everywhere. On the mantelshelf stood last year's Christmas cards. The room was very untidy and several cushions lay scattered on the floor.

Catweazle stood in the middle of all the strangeness as the vicar tried to put him at his ease.

'Do sit down, old chap,' he said. 'I except you're all in.'

Catweazle sat in a large wickerwork chair.

'No, not that one, it's Shirley Temple's. I don't know where she's got to,' said the vicar looking round. 'She went out with Spencer Tracey, half an hour ago.'

A small bright-eyed cat crept out from behind the wastepaper basket.

'Talk of the Devil!' said the vicar with a smile.

'Which one?' said Catweazle.

'You must forgive the *ménage*,' said the vicar, 'but cats just seem to gravitate to the vicarage.' He pointed to two more sleeping on a cushion. 'Laurel and Hardy,' he said. 'Then there's Buster Keaton, Jean Harlow and the Marx Brothers, Groucho, Chico, and Harpo. But they're all out at the moment.' He picked up the little cat, 'Magical little thing isn't she?'

'Verily the cat bringeth magic,' replied Catweazle, wondering why the sorcerer should need so many familiars.

'I, too, have a familiar spirit,' he said, taking Touchwood from his pocket. The vicar looked at Touchwood with friendly interest. 'I say,' he said. 'What a splendid chap! How long have you had him?'

'Nine hundred years,' replied Catweazle proudly.

The vicar backed away, convinced he was dealing with a lunatic, and began nervously edging towards the telephone.

'I invoked the Spirits of the Brazen Vessel,' Catweazle explained.

'Oh, did you?' said the vicar putting down Shirley Temple as he reached his desk.

'But 'twas in vain, I flew not back, but sideways.'

The vicar began to dial 999.

'Where did your, er, journey begin?'

'Hard by the farm at Hexwood.'

The vicar stopped dialling and replaced the receiver. 'Hexwood? Near Westbourne? Do you work there?' he asked beginning to look in the directory.

'Nay my work is at Castle Saburac,' Catweazle replied.

'Castle Saburac?' said the vicar shaking his head. 'Thought I knew all the villages round here.'

Touchwood croaked loudly.

'Bless you,' said the vicar nervously. 'Ah, here we are! Hexwood Farm, G. A. Bennet. Westbourne 583,' and he dialled the number.

Carrot answered the phone at the farm.

'Hullo,' said the vicar.

'Hullo,' said Catweazle to the vicar.

'Who is that speaking?' asked the vicar.

'It is I,' said Catweazle, looking puzzled.

'Could I speak to Mr Bennet?'

'I know not,' said Catweazle looking round the room.

'Sssh!' said the vicar to Catweazle. 'My name is Potts.'

'Ssssh!' said Catweazle to the vicar. 'My name is Catweazle.'

'Will you be quiet!' said the vicar. 'No I didn't mean you, I'm sorry,' he said down the phone to Carrot.

Catweazle looked astonished. The sorcerer was talking nonsense.

'I'm the Vicar of Banden,' said the vicar to Carrot.

'And I am Catweazle,' said Catweazle convinced that the sorcerer was mad.

'Hang on,' said Carrot, and fetched his father to the phone.

'George Bennet here,' he said, picking up the receiver.

'Ah, Mr Bennet,' said the vicar. 'It's the Vicar of Banden.'

Catweazle looked round the room. He was getting angry. 'Where is the invisible one?' he asked.

'I wonder if you could help me,' said the vicar to Mr Bennet.

'Ask me anything, my brother,' said Catweazle.

The vicar held the mouthpiece close. 'I've got a man here with me who's out of his mind,' he whispered.

'You'll have to speak up,' said Mr Bennet at the other end of the line.

'It's difficult,' said the vicar. 'He's here in the room with me.'

Catweazle drew Adamcos and brandished the knife, wildly.

'O invisible Demon,' he called. 'I bid thee appear!'

'Put that knife down!' said the vicar loudly.

Mr Bennet began to get worried. 'Is he attacking you?' he asked.

'No, I think he's harmless,' said the vicar.

Catweazle put his knife away. 'If 'tis a friendly demon then all is well,' he said.

Ignoring him as best he could, the vicar continued to talk to Mr Bennet. 'Is there a village or hamlet near you called Castle Saburac?'

'Castle Saburac?' repeated Mr Bennet. 'I don't think so.'

At the mention of Castle Saburac, Carrot looked up. It was Catweazle! He hadn't disappeared at all! But what was he doing in Banden?

In the vicarage, Catweazle came closer and closer to the vicar, fascinated by the white thing he was holding up to his face.

'Dost conjure with a magic bone?' he asked.

'Here, have one of these, old man,' said the vicar nervously as he saw Catweazle standing beside him, and offered him a cigarette.

Catweazle sniffed it, put it in his mouth and swallowed it, while the vicar still struggled to find out who his troublesome visitor was.

'He says he comes from near your farm, so I thought you might be able to identify him.'

'Why talkest thou to that bone?' asked Catweazle.

'Phone, not bone,' said the vicar angrily.

Mr Bennet turned to Carrot, 'I think they're both mad,' he said.

Catweazle, unable to resist it any longer, grabbed the phone from the astonished clergyman and yelled down it, 'If thou art a Demon, then I will destroy thee!' Mr Bennet was nearly deafened.

Then the vicar managed to get the phone away from Catweazle. 'Sorry about that,' he said.

'Look, Vicar,' said Mr Bennet. 'We'll get this sorted out. I'll pop over as soon as I can. If he gets violent, I should phone for the police.'

He hung up. 'He says there's an old chap there who knows me or something, and that he's gone potty.'

'Are you going now, Dad?' asked Carrot anxiously.

'Well, not like this,' said Mr Bennet, who was in his farm clothes and needed a shave.

As his father went upstairs Carrot thought frantically how he could rescue Catweazle. Somehow he had to get him back to Castle Saburac. The old man was becoming an awful nuisance. Sooner or later his father was bound to find out about him. He was already beginning to wonder why Carrot spent so much time in the woods and why he was always so short of money.

He ran out into the yard, where Sam was bent over the engine of Apollo Twelve. The noise was deafening and clouds of smoke poured from the exhaust.

'Runnin' lovely now, she is,' Sam shouted over the engine.

'How about that spin your promised me?' shouted Carrot.

Sam put down the bonnet. 'You're on!' he said, grinning at Carrot. 'Where d'you want to go?'

'Banden church,' said Carrot.

'Whatever for?' said Sam as they got in.

'Well,' said Carrot. 'It's interesting. Early Perpendicular.'

'Is it?' said Sam as the car rattled out of the yard. 'She'll do forty down Long View hill,' he said proudly.

As they reached his cottage, Sam stopped Apollo Twelve and called to old Mrs Woodyard who sat dozing in the front garden, 'I'm going over to Banden, mother.'

'What for?' old Mrs Woodyard said, opening her eyes and sitting up.

'Taking Mr Bennet's boy to see the church.'

'I'll get my coat.'

'You don't want to come, mother!' called Sam. He turned sadly to Carrot. 'I can't do anything with her. She always has to come. 'Fraid you'll have to sit in the back.'

Mrs Woodyard had not figured in Carrot's rescue plan at all. It was going to make things doubly difficult.

With a black hat firmly jammed down over her ears and an overcoat buttoned up to her neck, she came down the path to the front gate.

'Time you weeded this path,' she said to Sam.

'Yes, Mum,' he said and helped her into the car. She brushed his arm aside. 'I ain't one of your fancy girls,' she said.

Sam, who was thirty-five and never went out with girls because his mother disapproved, sighed as he tucked a rug round the old lady.

'And not too fast, Sam,' she said, as Apollo Twelve moved off. By the time they got to Banden, however, she was fast asleep.

'How long are you going to be?' asked Sam quietly.

'Only about ten minutes,' Carrot replied, getting carefully out of the back. 'Why don't you go and have a pint in the pub over there?'

'Now that's what I call a great idea, Carrot,' said Sam, looking cautiously at his mother. 'She won't wake yet. It's the fresh air.'

Carrot watched Sam going towards the pub and after another look at the old lady asleep in the car, he ran off towards the vicarage.

He crept round to the back and peered in at the window. Catweazle was there all right. He stood clutching the telephone, while the vicar vainly tried to take it from him.

'Do stop playing with the telephone!' said the vicar.

Catweazle held it cautiously to his ear. 'I hear no voices,' he said. ' 'Tis the electrickery?'

'Yes, of course it is!' said the exasperated vicar. 'Now put it down!'

'Sunandum! Hurands! Saritap! Ottarim!' Catweazle yelled into the mouthpiece waving his hands in magical signs, but no voices answered him. Bitterly disappointed he passed the receiver back to the vicar.

'Oh great magician! Conjure more voices with thy telling bone.'

'But I keep telling you, it isn't magic.'

'Thou liest, false sorcerer,' said Catweazle, switching from flattery to abuse. 'Conjure the voices!'

'Keep calm,' said the vicar soothingly. 'It's only the phone!'

'Thou wilt not share thy knowledge,' said Catweazle angrily. 'The young wizard of Hexwood, he is my true brother.'

Carrot grinned as he heard this, and ran back to the car. He had to create a diversion if he was going to get Catweazle out of there.

'Mrs Woodyard! Mrs Woodyard!' he called, giving the old lady a gentle shake.

Sam's mother woke with a start and looked up at him.

'Where's Sam?' asked Carrot.

'Ain't he with you?' she said.

'No, I thought he'd be back by now,' said Carrot.

'Why, where's he gone?'

'To the vicarage.'

'The vicarage?' said Mrs Woodyard, now fully awake. 'What's he gone there for?'

Carrot looked mysterious. 'I don't know, he wouldn't say. Just said he had to see the vicar about something. To arrange things.'

'To arrange things?' said Mrs Woodyard, getting alarmed. 'My Sam?'

'Yes,' said Carrot.

'Was there a young woman with him?'

'I didn't see one,' said Carrot truthfully.

'I'll put a stop to this,' said Mrs Woodyard, struggling from the car and marching off towards the vicarage.

Carrot followed her, and as she went up to the front door, he slipped round the back to the study window. Catweazle had his knife out and was menacing the vicar. 'Give me the secret of the telling bone, thou simpering sackbut,' he demanded.

'You're getting worked up again,' said the vicar, backing away.

'Thou braying bolster! Thou black bee-hive!' said Catweazle, driving him against the wall. Then the front door-bell rang. The strange sound made Catweazle jump back in sudden alarm, and, seizing his chance, the vicar escaped through the door, and locked him in.

'Now the telling bone is mine!' said Catweazle in triumph as he sliced through the wire with Adamcos and put the receiver in his pocket.

'Here,' hissed Carrot through the window. 'Quick, before he gets back!'

Catweazle, secretly delighted to see Carrot again, climbed out of the window and swiftly they crept back to the car.

Meanwhile the vicar had opened the front door to Mrs Woodyard.

'Yes?' he said, still very flustered.

'Where's Sam?' said Mrs Woodyard grimly.

'Oh, is that his name?' said the vicar. 'Well, he's inside. Getting very excited I'm afraid.'

'Is he indeed?' said Mrs Woodyard, beginning to bridle.

'I've had a terrible time with him.'

'He didn't tell me he was going to do it.'

'Well, they don't, you know, if they really mean to.'

'He could have told me though, surely,' said Mrs Woodyard. 'I would have understood.'

'Understood?' said the vicar amazed.

'After all, I am his mother.'

The vicar looked at the old lady with horror. She was obviously mad as well.

'I thought that would surprise you!' Mrs Woodyard went on. 'Who's he going to marry?'

'Shirley Temple!' said the vicar, suddenly remembering his precious cats. 'He's locked in there with Shirley Temple!'

It was Mrs Woodyard's turn to look frightened. They gaped at each other for a moment, then Mrs Woodyard turned and hobbled back to the car as fast as she could, while the vicar ran back to the study.

Carrot had just hidden Catweazle in the back of the car when Mrs Woodyard came hurrying back from the vicarage, and Sam reappeared from the pub.

'Hullo, mother,' said Sam, surprised to see the old lady awake.

'What have you been up to?' said Mrs Woodyard.

'Went for a pint,' said Sam, rather sheepishly.

Mrs Woodyard looked at both of them very suspiciously.

'Somebody's tellin' lies,' she said. 'I ain't got to the bottom of it yet, but I will.'

Carrot glanced anxiously down the road. 'Could we go back a different way, Sam?' he asked. He didn't want to meet his father on the road.

'Good idea,' said Sam, helping his mother into the car. 'Hope it starts.'

Apollo Twelve was hardly out of sight when Mr Bennet drove up to the vicarage and rang the bell.

The vicar opened the door at once. 'He's gone!' he said.

'The man you phoned me about?' said Mr Bennet.

'You're Bennet? How d'you do. Yes, gone. Vanished. Oh, do come in.'

'What was he like?' said Mr Bennet, as they entered the study.

'Oh, peculiar,' said the Vicar. 'And mad. Mad as a march hare. At least – ' He broke off, a sudden thought striking him.

'Well?' said Mr Bennet.

'Then this woman came. I wonder if it was all a trick to get me out of here.'

'I wish you'd explain,' said Mr Bennet.

'Suppose they were after the collection money!' gasped the vicar as he quickly opened his safe. 'No it's all here,' he said. 'But we'd better phone for the police.' He reached for the receiver. 'He's taken it with him!'

None of them were any the wiser what had happened. Mr Bennet returned home wondering if the vicar was mad, and so did Mrs Woodyard. Even Sam never realized that he had an extra passenger on the way home, for Catweazle managed to escape unseen when Apollo Twelve broke down a few miles from Hexwood and Sam crawled underneath to repair it. Only Carrot knew the whole story and he, of course, kept it to himself.

9

THE POWER OF ADAMCOS

CATWEAZLE sat on a fallen tree sharpening Adamcos. It was a calm and beautiful day in the wood and the magician was at peace. Beside him Touchwood sat motionless, patiently watching some gnats dancing above his head.

> 'Buzz quoth the blue fly,
> Hum quoth the bee,
> Buzz and hum they cry,
> And so do we'

sang Catweazle, honing his knife with a stone and occasionally testing the blade with his dirty thumb. When at last he was satisfied he carefully replaced Adamcos in its sheath round his neck.

'Now Adamcos,' he said, 'even thistledown shall fall to thy keen blade,' and he grinned his crooked grin.

He delved into his torn robe and took out the vicar's telephone. He had been trying for several days to conjure the spirits.

'Come, O magic telling bone,' he said, holding the receiver like a votive offering. 'Summon the voices!' and he placed the mouthpiece to his ear. 'Are you there Spirits? Are you there?'

There was silence. Touchwood, whose patience had been rewarded, gulped a gnat and regarded his master stonily.

'Come, Spirits,' commanded the old sorcerer testily. 'I charge thee, speak to Catweazle, Master of the Secret Path.'

'Thou shalt die!' said a voice.

Catweazle dropped the telephone in terror.

'Have at thee, villain!' said another voice.

Catweazle looked wildly round and suddenly realized that the voices did not come from the telling bone but from somewhere behind him. Cautiously he climbed on the fallen tree and peered through the bushes.

It was a Norman! He stood brandishing a long sword,

menacing a Saxon warrior who was desperately trying to defend himself.

Catweazle fell off the tree trunk in fear and amazement. He could hardly believe it but he was back in his own time again! Somehow it must have happened without his knowledge. His beard and whiskers trembled and picking up Touchwood he ran off in terror.

Had Catweazle looked longer, however, he would have seen Apollo Twelve standing on the road at the far edge of the clearing, and Sam, also dressed as a Norman, but wearing a sports coat over his chain-mail, bent over the engine.

With a yell, the Norman warrior dropped his wooden sword.

'Take it easy, Fred,' he said. 'That was my fingers!'

'Sorry, Dick,' said the Saxon.

'Stop foolin' about and give us a hand,' said Sam from the car. 'We're going to be late for the rehearsal.'

Every year, the Westbourne and District Operatic Society put on a pageant in the grounds of Old Westbourne House. It was produced by Stuffy Gladstone and the money raised was given to the Cottage Hospital.

'She was goin' a treat yesterday,' lied Sam, removing the sparking plugs.

'Reckon she's had it,' said Fred, taking off his helmet.

'I ain't walkin' five miles dressed like this,' said Dick.

Catweazle was still running blindly through the wood, but when he saw the old water tower in front of him he stopped and blew on his thumb-ring.

'My brain burns!' he moaned, 'Where am I? O Touchwood, Touchwood! The past and the present are one!'

He scrambled up into Castle Saburac and quickly drew a new circle round himself on the rusty plates of the water tank.

'O cursed telling bone!' he moaned, clenching his fists

and knocking his knuckles together in impotent rage and panic, 'thou hast brought Normans to plague me!'

He grabbed Rapkyn's book and searched through its ragged pages. 'I will bewitch them with flea-bane, blister them with hog-weed,' he said, vainly looking for a suitable spell.

He was still looking when Carrot climbed in with a rucksack full of supplies. ' 'Morning, Catweazle! 'Morning, Touchwood!' he said cheerfully.

'Hurry, earwig,' said Catweazle, hardly looking up from the book. 'Lest the Normans see thee.'

'I wish you'd shut up about the Normans,' said Carrot wearily. 'Once and for all, Catweazle, you are living in the twentieth century – '

'I believe thee, brother. I believe thee,' Catweazle interrupted. 'But there are Normans. I swear by – '

Catweazle looked down for Adamcos. The sheath was empty.

He dropped to the floor, making unhappy whimpering noises, and began scrabbling around like a dusty old crab.

'What's wrong now?' asked Carrot.

'Adamcos, 'tis gone!' cried the old sorcerer in a panic, 'Adamcos! Adamcos!'

'Don't moan,' said Carrot. 'We'll find it. You must have dropped it somewhere.'

By this time, Catweazle was making the most dreadful blubbering noise on the floor.

'For heaven's sake!' said Carrot. 'It's only a knife. Look, if you shut up, I'll buy you a new one.'

'Dost thou not know?' said Catweazle on all fours. 'Dost thou not understand? Without Adamcos I shall die!'

'What!' said Carrot.

'It holds the power of life. I shall perish if we find it not. At sunset I shall be no more!'

'I've never heard anything so daft,' said Carrot. 'Where did you have it last?'

'Hard by the Normans,' said Catweazle.

Carrot controlled himself with some difficulty. 'If you mention that word again I'll crown you,' he said.

'Crown? Me?' said Catweazle.

'Come on,' said Carrot. 'Let's go and find it.'

Catweazle followed Carrot very unwillingly back to the fallen tree, and nearly ran away when he heard voices, but Carrot grabbed him and pointed towards the road. He had seen Sam through the bushes.

'You idiot, Catweazle!' he grinned. 'They're not Normans. It's Sam! Today's the dress rehearsal for the show.'

Catweazle looked dazed. 'Show?' he said.

'Westbourne through the Ages,' explained Carrot. 'They do one every year. Dad's on the committee –'

'See, brother,' Catweazle broke in excitedly. 'Adamcos!'

Catweazle's knife lay in the pathway to the road. They were just worming their way forward to get it when they saw Mr Bennet coming and they had to hide behind the tree. He saw the knife on the path and took it across the clearing to show to Sam and the others who were still trying to start Apollo Twelve.

Catweazle and Carrot watched from their hiding-place.

'I say,' said Mr Bennet, 'does this belong to any of you?'

'Hullo, Mr Bennet,' said Sam. 'No, it ain't ours, is it boys?'

'Funny looking thing. Might be quite valuable,' said Mr Bennet.

'What's the trouble with the car?'

'I dunno,' said Sam, scratching his head.

'Died of old age probably,' said Mr Bennet. 'You'd better come back to the farm and I'll run you up to the house.'

'Thanks, boss,' said Sam.

'Carrot's supposed to number the seats. Haven't seen him, have you?'

Carrot crouched lower behind the tree trunk and none of the men spotted him as they turned back through the wood.

Catweazle began making his anxious little fizzing noises through his teeth, and Carrot glanced at him in alarm.

'I grow colder,' said Catweazle. 'I shall die!'

'It's imagination,' said Carrot, pulling him to his feet. 'Come on! We'll get it back somehow.'

They followed his father and the others back to the farm and watched them drive off in the farm truck, and then they began a frantic search of the house.

'I bet it's in the desk,' muttered Carrot, but it wasn't in any of the drawers.

'Come, Touchwood,' said Catweazle. 'Lead me to Adamcos.' He held the toad up and pointed him round the room like a torch. Suddenly, Touchwood croaked and Catweazle held his breath. Then the magician took a step forward in the direction Touchwood was pointing and Touchwood croaked again. Catweazle was convinced now that Touchwood knew what he was doing, and he went straight across the room, while Touchwood croaked harder and harder, until they finished up in front of a large china frog on the dresser.

'Thou art a fool,' said Catweazle to his familiar, and angrily put him back in his pocket.

Carrot came back from the sitting-room.

'Not in there either,' he said.

'What is to become of me?' moaned Catweazle.

'Don't start that again. You only think you're ill.'

Catweazle collapsed into a chair.

'There's nothing wrong with you. Get up,' said Carrot heartlessly, and pulled the sorcerer to his feet.

'My blood turns to ice!' moaned Catweazle, collapsing again. Carrot ran over to a cupboard and poured out some brandy. 'Here, have some of this,' he said, handing the glass to Catweazle.

' 'Tis a magic potion?' asked Catweazle hopefully.

'Yes. Drink it down fast. It'll warm you up.'

Catweazle tossed down the brandy. A look of surprise grew on his hairy face. Then as the drink took effect, he leapt to his feet.

'Yeeeeeaaaaaaaahhhhhhhh!' he cried, skipping round the room, clutching his stomach and then his throat. 'I burn! I burn!'

'Thought that would do the trick,' murmured Carrot.

Catweazle stopped jumping about and advanced on Carrot, coughing and spluttering. Tears ran down his face leaving little pale paths on his dirty face.

'Thou bow-legged beetle!' he snarled.

'That's better,' said Carrot.

'Thou white-legged worm!'

'Anything else?' asked Carrot calmly.

Catweazle took a deep breath. 'Thou wry-necked, trash-mongering, swaggering, double-tongued, huff-snuff!'

'Ten out of ten,' said Carrot.

'Thou art a Demon sent from hell to plague me,' said Catweazle, sitting down again.

'No I'm not,' said Carrot. 'I want to help you. We'll find Adamcos. I promise we will.'

'Before sunset?'

'Oh, yes,' said Carrot uneasily. 'Long before then.'

'Nay,' said Catweazle. 'I am doomed.'

'Well, you're supposed to be the magician. You ought to know where it is. You found the head of Cernunnos easily enough.'

Carrot suddenly stopped rummaging in the sideboard.

'Maybe we're wasting our time?'

'What meanest thou?'

'Maybe it isn't here at all. Suppose he's taken it into Westbourne with him?'

'Then let us follow,' said Catweazle, anxiously getting to his feet.

'But why would he do that?' wondered Carrot. 'Unless – '

Catweazle looked uneasily at Carrot, 'Unless – my brother?' he queried.

Carrot gulped. 'Unless he was going to sell it.'

Carrot had guessed right. After dropping Sam, Fred and Dick at Old Westbourne House, Mr Bennet had gone to see Leslie Milton, who ran the little local antique shop. He found Leslie sitting on his desk, a voluminous dress over his knees, surrounded by piles of costumes and large wickerwork baskets, trying hard to get the costumes finished in time for the dress rehearsal.

'I said last year, I'd never do it again,' he exclaimed. 'Forty-five costumes, Mr Bennet. I mean it's ludicrous, isn't it?' He took a tape measure from round his neck. 'Been up there yet?' he asked.

'I've just dropped Sam,' said Mr Bennet. 'I must say things seem pretty chaotic, but I suppose they'll get it sorted out eventually. How are you getting on?'

Leslie rolled his eyes upwards. 'Finished the last one at three this morning, apart from bits and bobs and poppers. Quite frankly, I'm dead!'

Leslie slid down from the desk and gave the dress to Mr Bennet. 'Just hold this a sec, will you?'

Mr Bennet held the dress up, feeling rather silly, while Leslie tried various coloured ribbons against it. Satisfied, he took back the dress and began sewing the ribbon into place.

'Whose is that one?' asked Mr Bennet.

'Mrs Thomas. Maid Marian. She had eight fittings. Thought I'd go berserk. Hope these seams hold.'

'Sam's wearing his already.'

'Well, I told the soldiers to come dressed. Thirty men changing in that tent would be like the black hole of Calcutta.'

Mr Bennet took Adamcos from his pocket and showed it to Leslie.

'Where did you get this?' asked the little man, examining it.

'I found it. Worth anything, do you think?'

'Wouldn't like to say. I'm more china and glass. Could be Art Nouveau. Why, d'you want to sell it?'

'Oh, no,' said Mr Bennet. 'You can have it. I wouldn't want Carrot fooling about with a thing like that, you see.'

'You are kind,' said Leslie, putting it round his neck. 'It's very bizarre.'

'Colonel Upshaw might like it. He collects daggers and spears. He's got another monkey you know.' Leslie knew all the local gossip. 'Thanks ever so much, Mr Bennet. By the way I've still got that decanter you liked.'

'I can't afford it at the moment,' said Mr Bennet hurriedly.

'Don't worry,' said Leslie. 'I keep it hidden behind Madam,' and he nodded towards a large picture of Sarah Bernhardt propped on a chest of drawers.

'I bought that in a moment of utter madness,' he said pointing to an Egyptian mummy case, standing in the corner. 'I'll never get rid of it. Gives me the creeps. You in a hurry Mr B.?'

'Well I – ' began Mr Bennet.

'I'm awful aren't I? I'd natter all day. Have I held you up?' said Leslie packing Mrs Thomas's costume in one of the baskets.

'No, of course not,' said Mr Bennet edging his way to the door. 'But I'd better go back to see if the Chairman's arrived yet.'

'Bye-bye, then,' waved Leslie. 'And thanks for the old dagger.'

Mr Bennet was hardly out of sight, before Carrot cycled up to the shop with Catweazle sitting on the carrier.

'Bet Dad brought it here,' said Carrot breathlessly. 'Mr Milton's an antique dealer.'

Catweazle followed him up to the door. 'Adamcos lies within?' he asked.

Carrot pointed glumly to a 'Closed' sign behind the glass.

' 'Tis a spell?' said Catweazle.

'No, it just means we can't get in,' said Carrot.

'O door!' said Catweazle, making signs at it, 'I charge thee, yield unto me!'

'Great burglar you'd make!' said Carrot, and then looked with surprise as the magician pushed open the door.

'See, poke-weed!' said Catweazle.

'How did you do that?' gasped Carrot.

'Ah!' said Catweazle, who didn't know.

They tiptoed inside and Catweazle brushed against a large vase on a stand. Carrot just managed to grab it before it toppled over.

'Whatever you do,' he whispered to Catweazle, 'keep quiet and don't break anything.'

He looked round wondering where to start. There were so many places Adamcos might be that it would take them hours to find it. Catweazle opened an ornamental box which immediately began to play 'The Bluebells of Scotland'.

'Why don't you just bang a gong and have done with it,' said Carrot and slammed it shut. At that moment he heard footsteps in the back room, and he only just had time to push the old man behind a high-backed chair, covered in costumes, before Leslie came into the room. He was carrying a pile of hats which concealed the fact that he was wearing Adamcos round his neck.

'Hullo, Carrot,' he said cheerfully, 'you've just missed your Dad.'

Carrot was surprised that Leslie should take the break-in so calmly.

'I thought you might be closed,' he stammered.

'I put the sign up to discourage customers. I'm so busy with all this, you see. But I didn't bother to lock the door.'

So much for magic, thought Carrot.

'Wouldn't like to help, would you?' asked Leslie, 'I must pop out for some bits. Could you stay and mind the phone?'

'Oh, yes, I'd be glad to,' said Carrot with alacrity.

Leslie breezed out and Carrot went over to the chair. Catweazle was shivering again.

'There is ice in my bones,' he said. 'My death draws nigh.'

'Don't give up,' said Carrot. 'I know we're going to find Adamcos.'

'I freeze,' croaked Catweazle.

Carrot looked at him worriedly. The old man's face was grey and drawn and he was trembling like a frightened dog. He had clearly made up his mind that he was going to die.

'You haven't got enough on,' said Carrot picking up a very choice pair of combinations from a pile of costumes. Leslie had dyed them pale green so that they could be worn under a tabard instead of tights.

'Put these on,' said Carrot firmly, anticipating resistance.

'What is it?' said Catweazle in horror.

'Coms. Combinations. A vest and long pants all in one,' explained Carrot. 'They're jolly warm.'

Catweazle climbed fearfully into the combinations and Carrot was just buttoning them up, when he saw the farm truck pull up outside. In a panic he pushed the protesting Catweazle inside an empty clothes skip and sat down on the lid just as his father and Sam came in.

'Oh, there you are,' said his father. 'I thought you were supposed to be numbering the seats?'

'Not yet,' said Carrot. 'I'm minding the phone for Mr Milton.'

'Isn't he here? Mr Gladstone's getting in a panic about the rest of the costumes. We've come to take all these skips up to the house.'

For a moment it looked as if they meant to take the one containing Catweazle but Carrot didn't budge, so Mr Bennet and Sam picked up one of the others and carried it out to the truck.

'Come out,' Carrot whispered to Catweazle as he jumped off the skip.

'Nay,' said Catweazle looking up at him.

'They'll be back in a second!'

'I care not.'

'Well I do,' said Carrot, hauling him out and looking round for somewhere to put him. With a flash of inspiration, he pulled open the old mummy case and just managed to get Catweazle safely stowed away before the two men came back.

'You'd better wait for Leslie,' his father said to him as they took the final skip. 'Then come up to Westbourne House.'

'Right, Dad,' said Carrot, breathing a sigh of relief as the farm truck drove away.

'Out you come,' he said to the mummy case.

There was a sudden frenzied knocking from within.

'Push, you idiot!' said Carrot.

A frantic mumbling came from inside.

'I can't hear you,' said Carrot.

There was more loud mumbling accompanied by wild banging.

'You'll have to speak up,' said Carrot, grinning.

But when he tried to open the mummy case he found that it had stuck.

'He'll suffocate,' muttered Carrot, and he grabbed a sword from the wall and attempted to lever the case open. As he did so, the whole thing began to rock to and fro till finally it fell over backwards, landing, with a sickening thud, face upwards on the floor.

'Catweazle,' said Carrot, kneeling beside it, 'say something.'

There was silence from the mummy case, but Leslie, who had heard the crash, came rushing into the shop.

'Whatever's happened?' he said.

Carrot looked up suddenly and saw Adamcos round the antique dealer's neck.

'Adamcos!' he exclaimed.

'Come again?' said Leslie, completely bewildered.

Slowly the lid of the mummy case began to open. Leslie stared at it with amazement, turning to terror as the lid fell back and a very dazed Catweazle rose up in his pale green coms, groaning most horribly, his beard and hair covered with thick dust.

Leslie took one look at the apparition and slid down the wall in a dead faint. Carrot pounced on Adamcos and restored it to Catweazle, who was still feeling pretty faint himself.

The effect was magical. Feeling his sacred knife once more, Catweazle jumped briskly out of the mummy case, picked up his robe and ran out of the shop with hardly a backward glance at Carrot. He didn't stop running until he was safely back in Castle Saburac.

'Did you see it? Did you see it?' said Leslie, coming round.

'See what?' said Carrot.

'The thing! The thing from the tomb!'

'You've been overworking, Mr Milton,' said Carrot innocently.

10

THE HOUSE OF THE SORCERER

SAM WOODYARD had worked at Hexwood for twelve years. He hated the turkeys and he wasn't very interested in farming, but he was reliable, even tempered and generally got on well with everyone. He was a good foreman and an expert with the farm machinery. Whenever anything broke down, Sam was always the one who would get it going again, so it was a shock when he came to Mr Bennet one morning and told him he was leaving.

'But why, Sam?' said Mr Bennet, absolutely flabbergasted.

'Well ... er ... I want a change I reckon,' mumbled Sam, looking at the floor.

'I thought you liked working here,' said Mr Bennet.

'Well, I do, I mean, I did,' stammered Sam. 'But, you see Mr Bennet, I ain't done anything. I ain't bin anywhere.'

'But why suddenly now?' asked Mr Bennet, bewildered.

'Well, I was never cut out for farming,' answered Sam, evasively.

'I've never heard anything so stupid,' said Mr Bennet. 'You're – '

'So I'm stupid am I?' interrupted Sam angrily.

'I didn't say that,' said Mr Bennet, 'I only meant that – '

'I'd be stupid to stay here,' said Sam, cutting in again, 'There ain't no future in it!'

There was a pause while Mr Bennet looked coldly at him.

'Are you implying I don't know how to run this farm?'

'I didn't say that,' said Sam. 'I only meant that – '

'Because when I want your opinion,' Mr Bennet went on rudely, 'I'll ask for it.'

'You never listen!' roared Sam, losing his temper completely.

'Don't shout,' shouted Mr Bennet.

'I ain't shouting,' shouted Sam. 'Don't tell me what to do!'

'I'll tell you what you can do right now, Woodyard,' shouted Mr Bennet. 'You can get out. You're fired!'

'Oh no I'm not,' said Sam. 'I'm giving notice! I've got a much better job,' and he slammed out of the door.

It was really all Cyril Fitton's fault. He had come down to Westbourne to record all the birds and animals of the area and had managed to persuade Sam to join him as his assistant. Cyril went all over the world with his caravan recording things and it was this tempting fact that had eventually made Sam decide to give up his job at the farm.

As he approached the clearing where Cyril's caravan stood, he was unaware that his old adversary Catweazle was watching from the safety of a convenient tree. Catweazle had been keeping a close watch on Cyril's activities for several days. He had heard terrible roarings coming from the little house but, when he screwed up the courage to peep through the window, all he could see was the sorcerer, wearing giant ears and bending over a sinister machine. At other times, the sound of wild music could be heard, doubtless played by invisible Demons, he thought fearfully.

Now, as Sam went inside, Catweazle couldn't resist creeping up to the window to see what was going on but unfortunately Cyril had drawn the curtains. Suddenly there was a strange high-pitched gabbling followed by a blood-curdling scream, and Catweazle took to his heels with a moan of terror.

'Startling, isn't it?' said Cyril switching off the tape-recorder. 'A screech owl of course. Bagged it in the Orkneys – took me a month. Finished up in hospital, suffering from exposure and malnutrition. Like to hear it again?'

'No thanks, Mr Fitton,' said Sam, taking some batteries from his pocket and putting them on the table. 'Those the right ones?'

'Good, good,' said Cyril, absorbed in adjusting the recording machine.

'I've chucked my job in at the farm,' said Sam.

'You won't regret it.'

'Hope not.'

'You'll love Iceland. I was there last spring with my ... er, former assistant.' Cyril stopped and stared into space. 'Unfortunate business that.'

'What was?' said Sam.

'Well, we were recording in a volcano,' said Cyril, shaking his head sadly.

Sam was horrified, 'You mean he – ?'

'Poor Jasper,' said Cyril. 'I've got the recording somewhere,' and he reached up to find it.

'I'd rather not,' gulped Sam hastily.

'Of course,' said Cyril. 'After all it's not as if you knew him. Here!' and he held up the microphone. 'Go on, say something.'

'Hullo,' said Sam feebly, still thinking about Jasper and the volcano.

'Louder,' said Cyril.

'This is Sam Woodyard speaking,' said Sam clutching the microphone as if his life depended on it.

'Good, good,' muttered Cyril, 'much more volume. Found anyone for "Vanishing Britain" yet?'

This was a set of folk-tales that Cyril was collecting from old people.

'Had a word in the pub last night,' said Sam putting

down the microphone. 'Wally said he might come up – he's a laugh.'

'Is he an octogenarian?' asked Cyril.

'I think he's a Methodist,' said Sam. 'But he knows lots of songs and jokes.'

Cyril sighed. Obviously Sam hadn't understood what he was looking for.

'You see,' he explained, 'some old people are positive treasure houses of folk material.'

'Are they?' said Sam. 'By the way, I found out where them badgers live, Mr Fitton.'

A plane roared overhead and Cyril leapt from his chair. He shook his fist in the air and a maniacal gleam appeared in his eyes.

'Aeroplanes,' he screamed in fury, 'aeroplanes!'

Sam watched him nervously while the noise of the plane died away, and Cyril gradually calmed down.

'Sorry about that,' said Cyril. 'I can't stand them. They ruined my only recording of the Yellow Bellied Sap Sucker.'

'We'll build a "hide",' he said, passing Sam a spade, 'and then they won't know we're there.'

'What, the planes?' said a rather worried Sam.

'No, of course not. The badgers,' said Cyril irritably.

'But I haven't brought me boots,' said Sam, who loathed digging.

'You can have Jasper's,' said Cyril, handing them to him. Sam put them on gingerly.

'Onward,' said Cyril, and led the way out of the caravan.

In the meantime Catweazle had reached Castle Saburac, where Carrot was anxiously waiting to tell him all about Sam leaving the farm.

'Oh my brother,' gasped Catweazle, very out of breath, ' 'Tis terrible, 'tis horrible! In the woods – a savage sorcerer – with great ears – on wheels!'

'Ears on wheels?' said Carrot, who was getting used to Catweazle's outbursts by this time.

'Gibbering fiends!' said Catweazle. 'Killing! Murdering! Save me, my brother! Save me!'

'Get up, Catweazle,' said Carrot sharply.

'Gab, gaba, agaba!'

'Calm down!'

Catweazle recovered his breath and sat down in the middle of his magic circle with all his fingers crossed.

'Thy Sam is no more,' he announced finally.

'What?' said Carrot.

'The foul fiend hath devoured him.'

'What are you talking about?'

'There is a sorcerer in the woods, brother. He liveth in a little house with wheels. He hath a cloak like a wheel.' Catweazle was referring to the large umbrella that Cyril used when he was recording in the rain.

'Then thy Sam cometh,' Catweazle stopped, overcome by the memory of the screams.

'Go on,' said Carrot, who was beginning to get interested.

'He goeth in.'

'Yes?'

'Oh my brother!' said Catweazle, burying his face in his hands, 'the screams, the dreadful screams!'

'You're imagining things,' said Carrot. 'Why would anyone want to kill Sam? Where is this caravan?'

'Nay he will kill us all,' said Catweazle.

'Just show me where it is.'

Catweazle shook his head vigorously.

'Look, Catweazle,' said Carrot trying to reason with him. 'You've probably got it all wrong anyway, but even if you haven't, two magicians ought to be able to fix this new bloke.'

'Bloke?' muttered Catweazle.

'Two sorts of magic are better than one, aren't they?'

'Mayhap, mayhap,' said Catweazle cautiously. 'But first, brother, widdershins!'

'What?' said Carrot.

'Widdershins, brother!' said Catweazle impatiently. 'Widdershins!'

'What are you babbling about?' said Carrot.

'We must seek protection. Dost not know widdershins?'

'No,' said Carrot.

' 'Tis beyond belief,' said Catweazle, shaking his head.

Spreading his arms, the old sorcerer crouched down and began to revolve on the spot. Faster and faster he whirled until he was spinning like a top. The whole tank began to shake and Carrot clutched hold of a girder to steady himself. As he whizzed round and round, Catweazle began to hum until the noise was deafening. Finally, unable to keep his balance, he collapsed in a heap on the floor.

' "Round and round, the charm is wound",' he gasped. 'Now I am ready.'

'You look ready,' laughed Carrot, helping the dizzy magician to his feet. Catweazle fumbled in his robe and held up Touchwood, who looked somewhat greener than usual.

'Come, my warrior,' said Catweazle fiercely. 'Let us into battle!'

Touchwood croaked feebly and his eyes bulged.

'He's a bit small for a battle, isn't he?' said Carrot as Catweazle began to climb up the ladder.

'He may be small, brother, but he hath the spirit of a lion. Thou shalt see! To arms, Touchwood!' cried Catweazle, now apparently ready for anything. 'To arms!'

Carrot could barely restrain him as they reached the clearing and caught their first sight of the caravan.

'See,' said Catweazle, ' 'tis the house of the sorcerer.'

Carrot was puzzled. What was a caravan doing in the woods?

'Are you sure it was Sam?' he asked.

'I know the clodpole,' nodded Catweazle.

Together they crept up to the side of the caravan. The curtains made it impossible to see inside but a further investigation showed Carrot that the door was ajar.

'Nay, brother,' whispered Catweazle, restraining him. 'Enter not – 'tis a trap!'

Carrot went inside all the same. He was amazed by all the microphones and tape-recorders and a map of the world on one wall, on which Cyril had stuck little coloured flags at all the places he had made recordings. To Carrot, who often read spy stories, the whole thing seemed very suspicious. Then he spotted Sam's shoes and stared at them in horror.

'Catweazle!' he called in a loud whisper.

The magician crept in.

'Look!' said Carrot. 'They're Sam's!'

' 'Tis so,' nodded Catweazle.

'But he can't be – ' Carrot was unable to finish the sentence.

'My thumbs prick,' muttered Catweazle. 'Someone comes!'

Through the back window they were appalled to see Cyril returning from the 'hide'. He was carrying the spade over his shoulder.

Now Carrot was really scared. He darted out and ran for the shelter of the trees, but Catweazle caught his robe on a hook and by the time he had freed himself, it was too late for escape. Taking refuge in the wardrobe, he waited, trembling, as Cyril entered the caravan. Unfortunately, Touchwood found the strong smell of mothballs disturbing and began to croak loudly.

Cyril flung open the door.

'What on earth d'you think you're doing in there?' he said, looking with distaste at Catweazle who was blowing furiously on his thumb-ring.

'Spare me!' he pleaded.

'Have you taken anything?'

Catweazle shook his head.

'You haven't touched any of this?' said Cyril, looking anxiously at his beloved tape-recorders. Catweazle shook his head again, too frightened to speak.

'Well, come on man, what are you doing here?'

'S-S-S-Sam,' Catweazle managed to stammer.

'Sam?' repeated Cyril, very puzzled. 'Oh, I see!' he went on, suddenly smiling. 'You must be Wally! You've come to record!'

Catweazle had no idea what the sorcerer was talking about.

'Your courage deserted you, so you hid in the wardrobe,' smiled Cyril as he switched on a tape-recorder. 'Well don't worry, it's quite painless,' and he chuckled at his own feeble joke, as he reached for a pad.

'I'd better have a few details before we start. Now then, Mr . . . What's your name?'

'Catweazle,' said the magician.

'Wally Catweazle,' wrote Cyril. 'How old are you?'

Catweazle was just going to say, 'Nine hundred years,' but thought better of it and remained silent.

'Forgotten eh? Never mind, just tell me all about yourself,' Cyril continued, putting a microphone in front of Catweazle, who eyed it fearfully.

'Pretend it isn't there,' said Cyril and wound the tape forward at high speed. Hearing the eerie chattering sound again, Catweazle made for the door, but Cyril grabbed him and forced him down into the chair.

'Wilt thou murder me?' cried Catweazle.

'Of course I won't,' said Cyril patiently. 'I want to

record you, don't you understand. For posterity. You are part of an England that has gone.'

'Ay, 'tis true,' said Catweazle sadly. 'Long gone.'

'You see,' said Cyril. 'I want you to take me back into the past.'

'Nay, master,' Catweazle replied. 'I have tried and tried in vain.'

Cyril looked puzzled at this. Perhaps the old man's mind was going, he thought. Then, in order to allay Catweazle's fears, he began to explain just how he made a recording.

'The tape goes past the head, you see,' he said. 'And you press this button when you want to wind back.'

'Wind back!' repeated Catweazle excitedly. 'Wind back!'

'Er ... yes,' said Cyril watching him nervously. 'Shall we begin?'

'Wilt thou wind me back?' asked Catweazle eagerly.

'As soon as we've finished.'

Cyril bent over the machine and put on a pair of head-phones. Catweazle quaked when he saw the giant ears again and looked so odd that he made Cyril press the wrong button.

'This is Sam Woodyard speaking,' said the tape recorder.

Catweazle leapt up, pointing a quivering finger at the machine.

' 'Tis he?' he cried.

'Yes, of course,' said Cyril removing his head-phones. 'Now for heaven's sake sit down. I'm going to put you on there as well.'

With a great shriek, Catweazle clutched the tape and broke it. Cyril jumped up and tried to restrain him, but the forward wind button became pressed during the struggle and tape shot off the spinning spool and began to wrap itself round the two of them. As they flailed about, Catweazle sat on the other tape-machine and immediately the sound of an express train filled the caravan. This was enough for Catweazle. As the express train began blowing its whistle, he broke free and tore out of the caravan, festooned with tape, while Cyril sank on to the steps, and covered his face with his hands.

Back at the farm, Carrot had found his father on the phone trying hard to get a replacement for Sam.

'Sam's been murdered!' yelled Carrot, as he burst in. 'Look!' and he held up the shoes.

'For heaven's sake Carrot!' said Mr Bennet. 'I'm on the phone!'

'He's buried in the woods!' Carrot went on breathlessly.

'Will you go away?' asked Mr Bennet putting his hand over the mouthpiece. 'I'm sorry, Ken, what were you saying?'

'You've just got to believe me, Dad,' said Carrot desperately. 'Sam's dead I tell you!'

'I'll phone you back,' said his father into the phone. 'Now listen Carrot –' he continued as he hung up.

'It's true Dad. Murdered! These are his shoes. I found them in the caravan.'

Mr Bennet looked at his son's worried face and took him into the kitchen.

'Now sit down,' he said. 'Suppose you tell me this whole thing right from the beginning.'

'There's this caravan,' said Carrot. 'In the woods, by Kingfisher lake. And we – I – went in and found these shoes and I know they're Sam's and the man buried him in the wood and he's some sort of spy.'

'Now just a moment –'

'The place is full of radio equipment and there's a map on the wall with flags and things. Sam must have found out, and that's why he left us. He was trying to run away. But they got him!'

'Is that the lot?' said Mr Bennet. 'Have you finished?'

The door opened and Sam walked into the kitchen.

'Are you a ghost?' said Carrot, open-mouthed.

Sam looked bewildered. 'Don't be daft, Carrot,' he said. He turned to Mr Bennet. 'I come to apologize, boss,' he said. 'Wouldn't have me back would you?'

Mr Bennet was only too delighted and apologized too, and while a rather shamefaced Carrot made some tea, Sam told them all about Cyril.

'Finished up sitting in a hole waitin' for him to record some badgers, but he never came back. Reckon I was always meant to work on a farm anyway,' said Sam, with a sigh.

11

THE CHANGELING

ONE morning, Catweazle returned to Castle Saburac from a foraging expedition to find Carrot waiting for him.

'Come here,' said Carrot grimly.

Catweazle did as he was told, looking somewhat sheepish.

'What have you been up to?' asked Carrot.

There was a pause and Catweazle glanced at two turkeys sitting on a nest of straw in the corner of the tank.

'Thou art a prying ferret,' he said defensively.

'And you're a thieving old rascal!' said Carrot, exploding. 'What about these turkeys?'

'I found them,' said Catweazle brazenly.

Carrot sighed. When would he understand about stealing?

'You'd pinch one of the cows if you could get it up here,' said Carrot. 'I try to help you, don't I? I mean, look at all the bananas I've bought! It's costing me a fortune.'

'Ay, thou art good to my belly,' said the magician. 'But thou wilt not share thy magic,' he added.

This was an old argument. 'It's not magic, it's Science,' said Carrot patiently, 'I've told you so, many times.'

'Words! Words!' snapped Catweazle, 'Men fly and 'tis not magic? Dost think me a fool? Tell me the secret of the electrickery!'

'You wouldn't understand,' said Carrot wearily.

Catweazle's beard quivered with fury. 'Presumptuous

pin!' he raged. 'I am Catweazle, Master of the Mysteries, I understand all things. Give me thy electrickery!'

'You can't have it!' shouted Carrot, also losing his temper. 'And if I catch you pinching again, I'll turn you in.'

'Into what?' said Catweazle, suddenly apprehensive.

'Just in,' warned Carrot as he left, throwing down a large bunch of bananas.

Catweazle fumed as the young sorcerer disappeared. 'Thou spider's spittle,' he muttered to himself as he picked up Rapkyn's book, 'I will confound thee.' A spell of really extraordinary power had to be fashioned, one that would enchant the Hexwood wizard and turn him into something very nasty, perhaps a slug or even a flea.

Presently he found the spell he was looking for and began to prepare. He rummaged among a collection of herbs and dried plants and produced a strange twisted root. It looked almost like a tiny man. Next he tied nine knots in a short length of string, and sprinkled some dead flies into the fire.

'Take thou a mandrake,' Catweazle read from the book. 'Mandrake, 'tis good,' he said as he picked up the root.

'Bind the root, with a witch ladder,' he held up the knotted string. 'Saying the while . . .' Catweazle squinted at the cabalistic symbols in the book. 'Ah, Rapkyn, thy writing is a poor scrawl,' he complained. 'Saying the while:

> A hog, a dog, a bat, a cat,
> A vole, a mole, a pig, a rat.
> As these knots bind thee tight,
> Be thou now the one I spite.'

Catweazle wound the string tightly round the root.
'Change thou thy shape,' he commanded. Then hold-

ing the root over the fire he spun it round and round. 'Zazas. Zazas. Natansandas. Zazas,' he cried.

He felt a twinge of shame at first that he should have made such a spell, especially against his brother in magic. Then he remembered how Carrot had refused to share the electrickery and, growing angry again, he hoped the spell would have a devastating effect.

He was relaxing after his efforts and absently eating a banana when a small monkey climbed down the ladder into the tank.

Catweazle had never seen a monkey before and he scuttled away from it in fear while the two turkeys ran about uttering gobbling cries of alarm, their necks turning all the colours of the rainbow. Quite unperturbed the monkey picked up Catweazle's banana and began to eat.

Catweazle watched it, and trembled. He drew Adamcos and waved it at the monkey. 'Avaunt, thou goblin!' he cried. 'Gab, gaba, agaba!'

The monkey took no notice and went on eating the banana.

'What devil art thou?' Catweazle inquired in a quavering voice.

The monkey finished the banana and threw the skin at Catweazle.

Slowly it began to dawn on the magician who the creature might be.

'Art thou ...? Art thou ...?' stammered Catweazle. But the monkey said nothing.

The spell had worked! Catweazle was triumphant. He had turned the young sorcerer into this hairy gnome with the long tail! 'See, Touchwood,' he said, 'how strong was the spell! 'Tis our brother!' But Touchwood, who didn't like the look of the monkey at all and had already had enough of the turkeys, tried to wriggle from his master's grasp.

'Canst thou not speak?' Catweazle said to the monkey, and the monkey bared its teeth and jumped up and down.

'I warned thee of my power, thou disbelieving dribblet.'

Catweazle looked closely at the monkey. 'Thou art a strange beast,' he said, twisting his forefinger in his beard with wonder. 'Yet I would know thee. Thou hast thy look. Thou art but half-changed. A demi-devil.'

The monkey, who had calmed down now, like the rest of the menagerie, allowed Catweazle to pick him up, and immediately began to groom his whiskers.

Catweazle sat on one of the boxes and cradled the monkey in his arms. 'Mock me now, thou hairy thing,' he said gleefully, and Touchwood crawled away in disgust.

'If thou art good to me, I'll change thee back,' Catweazle promised the monkey. 'Thou shalt be as thou wert,' and he sat back, highly pleased with the success of his spell.

Carrot, who was quite unaware that he had been turned into anything, had reached home to find Colonel Upshaw, whose land adjoined the farm, talking to Sam and his father.

'You haven't seen him, have you?' said the colonel, very red in the face.

'Who?' said Carrot, worried that Catweazle had been discovered.

'My monkey,' explained the colonel.

'Oh, no,' said Carrot with relief.

'I was dustin' me stuffed rhino when it happened,' said the colonel. 'Opened the cage, the cunning little beggar. Skipped out before I could catch him.'

'We haven't seen him,' said Mr Bennet.

'Didn't think you would have, George,' said the colonel. 'Just thought I'd check. Would happen today with Nathaniel Wheeler coming down. He's lecturin' at Breckley and I'm entertainin' him.'

'Not the explorer?' said Carrot, who had read every book Nathaniel Wheeler had written.

'That's right,' said the colonel. 'Like to meet him?'

'Gosh! Yes!' said Carrot.

'Pop round about six then. You too, George.' The colonel stood up. 'If you see Boy, give me a ring, will you?'

'Boy?' said Mr Bennet.

'My monkey,' said the colonel as he went off to search the surrounding woods. He stopped occasionally and fired his gun in the air, hoping to scare the monkey from its hiding-place. Catweazle heard the sound of firing in Castle Saburac, where he was failing miserably in an attempt to reverse his spell. Poking his head out of the inspection hole, he looked down at Colonel Upshaw as he went past firing the gun.

'A mighty magician,' gasped Catweazle, when he recovered from the deafening bang. 'Mayhap he will change thee back,' he said, picking up the monkey and putting him carefully inside a large cardboard box. 'Come, my brother, he that hath the thunder stick shall change thee, and help me return to my forest.'

He followed Colonel Upshaw all the way home and watched him disappear into his conservatory. The colonel called it 'The Jungle' because it reminded him of Africa. It was hot and steamy and full of luxuriant tropical plants.

He looked at the empty cage. 'Boy's really gone this time, Coote,' he said sadly to his housekeeper, Miss Coote. 'No sign of him.'

'He's answered the call of the wild, Colonel,' said Miss Coote, putting a cloth on the table.

'Don't be soft, he was born in Harrods,' replied the colonel shortly.

Miss Coote blushed and busied herself laying the table.

'Have you watered?' asked the colonel, propping his gun against the wall. Miss Coote stopped laying the table, and blushed again. She had completely forgotten.

'Not good enough, Coote,' said the colonel. He pointed at a giant plant. 'Look at poor old Ansittium Funicularis. Absolutely parched.' Miss Coote ran to fetch a watering can.

'No, no, I'll do it,' said the colonel impatiently. 'It'll take my mind off Boy.'

Miss Coote hurried away into the sitting-room and the colonel picked up a hose pipe and fixed it on a tap near the door. As he disappeared among the plants, spraying them gently with the hose, Catweazle came in from the garden carrying the monkey in the cardboard box.

The hose fascinated him and so did the tap. Was this electrickery he wondered, and turned it full on. There was a yell from Colonel Upshaw as the full force of water bounced off a flowerpot and hit him in the face. Unable to control the hose which was now like a writhing snake, he charged round the plants spraying water everywhere.

'You blithering idiot!' roared the colonel, skidding on the wet tiles, 'what on earth d'you think you're doing?'

'I am Catweazle,' said the magician, avoiding the water as much as he could.

The colonel turned off the tap and straightened up, his glasses running with water. 'Nat Wheeler?' he gasped. 'Good Lord! My dear chap! You're soaked, absolutely soaked!'

He took off his glasses and tried to wipe them. 'I'd no idea it was you. Thought you were comin' down later. Must be somethin' wrong with that tap. Coote! Coote! he called into the sitting-room.

He turned to Catweazle. 'Must find something for you to change into,' he said.

Catweazle looked at him with horror. He had no wish to be changed into anything. He had seen what his own experiment had led to. Nevertheless he was forced to take off his wet robe and put on a pair of Colonel Upshaw's cricket trousers and a navy blazer.

When eventually they returned to the conservatory, Miss Coote had lunch ready. Catweazle picked up the box and handed it to the colonel.

'Oh, you shouldn't have done this,' said the colonel, thinking it was a present. He was staggered when the monkey jumped out.

'It's Boy,' he cried, recognizing his pet.

'Ay,' said Catweazle miserably, ' 'tis the boy indeed!'

'Amazin',' said the colonel, who was really completely bewildered. 'How did you find him?'

'With a mandrake root,' said Catweazle.

'Oh, really?' said the colonel. 'I always use bananas.'

'End his misery,' said Catweazle who wanted to see Carrot changed back again. 'I know thou canst. Thou hast the Power,' and he pointed to the thunder stick.

The colonel was astounded. Why on earth did Wheeler want him to shoot his pet? 'But there's nothing wrong with him!' he said, putting the monkey in the cage.

'There you are, Boy,' he said, coming out of the cage and carefully shutting the door. 'What makes you think he's not himself?' he asked Catweazle.

Catweazle was regretting everything. He had hoped this sorcerer would help him. But instead of changing the young wizard back again, he had imprisoned him, and clearly intended to leave him in his devilish form.

'Sit down old chap,' said the colonel. 'So glad you could come,' he continued, pouring a glass of wine for Cat-

weazle. 'The skin off your nose,' he said cheerfully.

Catweazle grabbed his nose. The skin was still there. He sniffed at the wine, in case it was poisoned.

'I can see you like a good claret,' said the colonel, 'Château Margot, '59.'

'Shattow Margow Fifty-nine,' said Catweazle repeating what he took to be a spell. Slowly, as he drank the wine, an expression of bliss spread over his gnarled face. He had never tasted anything as good before. So this was what the sorcerers drank in this strange new world! He swallowed the wine happily and eagerly held out his glass for more while Colonel Upshaw talked on and on about Africa. At last Catweazle had drunk nearly three bottles of claret. As fast as Colonel Upshaw filled his glass, Catweazle drank it, and as he drank, he became more and more belligerent until with a truculent glare, he picked up the lid of a tureen in one hand and the carving knife in the other and menaced the colonel with them.

'Release the boy!' demanded Catweazle, weaving unsteadily.

'Now, now, old chap,' said Colonel Upshaw, somewhat taken aback, 'stop foolin' about. Boy's all right where he is.'

'Release him!' said Catweazle, waving the carving knife.

'Ha, ha,' laughed the colonel, nervously. 'Put it down, there's a good fellow.'

'Thou saucer-eyed pig's bladder!' shouted Catweazle making a sudden lunge.

'Coote! Coote!' called Colonel Upshaw, suddenly panicking. 'Wheeler's run amok!'

'Call thy witch!' cried Catweazle recklessly. 'Thou hast no power over me!'

'You've taken too much on board,' said the colonel.

'Thou bodkin!' said Catweazle as Miss Coote appeared.

'He's fighting drunk,' warned the colonel.

Catweazle staggered as the walls seemed to spin round him.

'I am bewitched,' he cried, dropping the carver with a clatter.

'Look out, Colonel!' screamed Miss Coote.

Catweazle gave a strange cry, rolled his eyes upwards and passed out with a thump at the colonel's feet.

'Kept on about wantin' to shoot Boy,' said the colonel. 'Couldn't make it out, Coote.'

'He seemed very unbalanced to me,' said Miss Coote, gazing down at the inert figure.

'Africa does something to a chap, you know,' said Colonel Upshaw winding up his ancient gramophone and putting on a very old record of the massed bands of the Grenadier Guards.

Catweazle remained unconscious on the conservatory floor all afternoon. He was still asleep when Mr Bennet and Carrot arrived.

Miss Coote ushered them into the sitting-room.

'George! Teddy!' said Colonel Upshaw enthusiastically. 'Nice of you to come. I'm afraid Wheeler's out at the moment.'

'Out?' queried Mr Bennet.

'Out cold, George. In there,' and he pointed to the adjoining conservatory. 'Very good year, the '59,' he added dryly.

'It must be,' smiled Mr Bennet. 'Did you find your monkey by the way?'

'Yes, well, that was a bit extraordinary,' said the colonel, 'because Wheeler brought him back.'

'Could I see him. The monkey I mean,' said Carrot.

'I suppose so,' said the colonel. 'Don't wake Mr Wheeler though. He'd better sleep it off.'

Carrot went into the conservatory and tip-toed to the cage. The door was open and he went inside, but the monkey was nowhere to be seen. Hearing a loud snoring snuffle Carrot looked round at the prostrate figure on the floor.

'Catweazle!' he gasped in a hoarse whisper.

The old magician opened his eyes. Standing in the cage, and quite his former self, stood the young sorcerer.

'Thou hast changed! Thou hast changed!' said Catweazle with wonder.

'Well, I thought I'd better,' said Carrot, who was wearing a suit in honour of Nathaniel Wheeler. 'What are you doing here? Where's the monkey?'

'Dost mean the sorcerer?' said Catweazle.

'Did you let it out?'

Catweazle stared blankly at Carrot and then as he heard voices approaching he ran over to the garden door, snatched up his robe and ran off through the rhododendron bushes.

Colonel Upshaw came into the conservatory carrying the monkey.

'He was behind my chair, all the time, Teddy. Must've got out again,' he whispered. 'Hullo, where's Wheeler?'

Mr Bennet joined them, and although they looked all over the garden they couldn't find the explorer. The colonel was about to contact the police when Miss Coote came up to tell him that Mr Wheeler had just phoned. He was sorry he was unable to come down and hoped he had not caused too much inconvenience.

'You're the mystery man, as far as Colonel Upshaw is concerned,' said Carrot, sitting with Catweazle in the candle-lit water tank later that night.

'I will not seek other magicians,' said Catweazle guiltily. 'I will not steal thy strange birds.'

'Good,' said Carrot, who had heard the whole story of his transformation and was not going to spoil things by explaining.

'I will not enchant thee again, I swear it,' said Catweazle in an agony of repentance.

'And no more monkey business?' said Carrot.

12

THE FLYING BROOMSTICKS

IT had been another busy day at the farm. Sam and Carrot had spent the morning transferring the latest batch of young turkeys from the tier brooders to the large specially heated sheds, and now everyone was hard at work on the orchard. Carrot and his father were loading the final baskets of apples on to the trailer when Sam, who had lit a bonfire to burn all the rubbish, accidentally set fire to his broom.

'Darn the thing,' he muttered as he hastily beat it out.

'Better damp that fire down,' said Mr Bennet. 'It's not safe.'

Sam did as he said and then swung himself on to the tractor. Carrot sat on the back of the trailer, and Mr Bennet watched as Sam drove carefully out of the gate. Then he picked up an apple, checked that the bonfire was safe, and prepared to follow them on foot.

A blue and white Panda car drew up as Mr Bennet reached the gate with Winston.

' 'Exwood Farm?' called a rather pasty-faced police sergeant, eyeing the dog nervously.

Mr Bennet nodded, his mouth full of apple.

'Are you Mr Bennet?'

'That's right,' said Mr Bennet, swallowing hastily.

'I've taken over from Sergeant Fulton,' explained the policeman, 'I'm new to the district, you see, sir. They sent me down here for a bit of a rest. I've bin over-doin' it a bit.'

He got out of the car and straightened his uniform.

'My name's Bottle, sir. Unfortunate name, isn't it? Wide open to ridicule. However, there it is.'

Suddenly, Sergeant Bottle spotted the burnt broom and he picked it up, carefully wrapping a handkerchief round it.

'They've struck again,' he muttered.

'I beg your pardon?' said Mr Bennet.

'Look at that, Mr Bennet, sir. Examine it. Do you notice anything peculiar about it?'

'Well, it's been burnt,' said Mr Bennet.

'Exactly,' said Sergeant Bottle. 'Burnt!' He sniffed at the broom. 'Recently burnt. This 'ere broom may be the vital link, especially if I can find out who burnt it.'

'Well, I can tell you that,' said Mr Bennet. 'My foreman burnt it.'

'Did he now, Mr Bennet,' said Bottle dramatically.

'Look, what's all this about?' asked Mr Bennet, who had never met a policeman quite like Bottle before.

'Well sir, it's a mysterious business. Not the sort of case I'm used to – comin' from the metropolis.'

'Perhaps you'd better come round to the farmhouse,' said Mr Bennet.

Bottle opened the car door. ' 'Op in, sir,' he said, putting the burnt broomstick in the back.

Carrot and Sam were beginning to store the freshly picked apples in the loft, when the police car drove into the yard.

'Bet he's after me,' muttered Sam.

'What for?' asked Carrot.

'Old Fulton would've just reminded me, but I don't know about this new feller. It's the car, you see. It ain't taxed. They were lookin' at her outside the market yesterday.'

'Think they'll summons you?' said Carrot.

'I dunno,' said Sam gloomily. 'I hope mother doesn't find out.'

As they watched, the two men below them passed Apollo Twelve and went into the barn.

Sergeant Bottle looked carefully round and then sat down heavily on a bale of straw. 'You see sir, it was only last week they started to go. I'd only been down 'ere three days.'

'What started to go?' said Mr Bennet, who was anxious to get back to his work.

'Brooms,' said Bottle darkly.

'Brooms?'

'Yes, Mr Bennet,' said Bottle consulting his notebook. 'Birch brooms or besoms as they're sometimes called. Eighteen from the Forestry. Four or five from private houses and ten from a Mr Rangi Lee's caravan. He makes 'em, you know,' he added.

'But it must be some form of practical joke,' said Mr Bennet.

'Ah!' said Bottle. 'That's what I thought at first. A hoax. But we recovered six of 'em today, and they was all burnt, and they was all tied together.'

'That is a bit odd,' admitted Mr Bennet.

'It's more than odd, it's sinister.'

Bottle came closer to Mr Bennet.

'You see, sir,' he said, 'underneath, *underneath* country people are still very primitive.'

'Oh, are they?' said Mr Bennet, who was a countryman born and bred.

'Yes sir, the veneer's quite thin you know. Superstition dies 'ard. Old beliefs linger.'

'Old beliefs?'

'Pagan rites,' breathed Bottle, producing a book called *Witchcraft Today*. On the cover was a witch dancing round a fire on a broomstick.

'Bin doin' some research,' said Bottle, tapping the book. 'Broomsticks you see. Fire. Unholy practices. The Black Mass.'

'The Black Mass?' repeated Mr Bennet with bewilderment.

'Don't worry. I've alerted the Vicar,' said Bottle. 'We may need him later on.'

'But Sergeant –'

'Who owns that old car outside?'

'Sam, my foreman,' explained Mr Bennet.

'The feller who burnt the broom?'

'That's right, but –'

'Then the net's tightening. That there car was seen near where we found the burnt brooms.'

'Now just a minute, Sergeant. First of all you tell me that someone's practising witchcraft and now you say it's Sam.'

'How else can you explain it?'

'But it's fantastic!'

'I agree, Mr Bennet. Nothing like this ever 'appened in Wimbledon.'

'But Sam's not the sort of chap to get mixed up in anything weird.'

'The most unlikely people get involved, Mr Bennet, according to this book. Cabinet Ministers, even Union Officials. Whatever you do – don't arouse his suspicions. He could turn very nasty. Just tell 'im I'd like to see 'im. You know, casual like. Give me time to get back to the station, and then send him along.'

And with that Sergeant Bottle rose, brushed the straw from his trousers, and marched back to his car.

When Mr Bennet climbed up into the apple loft, he wasn't quite sure how to tackle Sam.

'What did the policeman want, Dad?' asked Carrot, while Sam glared at him.

'Well, it's a bit difficult to explain,' said Mr Bennet uneasily. 'He wants to see you, Sam.'

'Ah well,' said Sam, 'I've bin expectin' it. They were bound to get me in the end.'

Mr Bennet was staggered.

'You mean, you admit it?' he said.

'Not much point in denyin' it,' said Sam.

'I can't believe it,' said Mr Bennet. 'I didn't think that sort of thing went on anymore. Not round here anyway.'

'Aw, there's thousands of people they never find out about. They won't shoot me,' said Sam.

'Well, you'd better get down to the station,' said Mr Bennet, very surprised at the calm way Sam was taking it.

'Thanks Mr Bennet, I'll go on my bike,' said Sam with a wink as he climbed down from the loft.

Mr Bennet was wondering what this last remark had meant when Carrot butted in.

'What's wrong, Dad?' he asked.

'Sam's in serious trouble, and he doesn't seem to realize it.'

'About Apollo Twelve?'

'I wish it was,' said his father. 'No, a lot of brooms have been stolen and then burnt. This man Bottle's got the idea that it's something to do with witchcraft. You know, Black Magic.'

'Black Magic!' gasped Carrot, thinking immediately of Catweazle.

'He's fairly convinced it's Sam,' Mr Bennet went on.

Carrot's mind was in a whirl. What was Catweazle up to now? He had to get up to Castle Saburac and find out. He waited until his father was busy in another part of the farm and then slipped away to the woods.

As he approached the water tower he saw Catweazle standing by a small bonfire reciting a complicated spell. Touchwood sat watching from a tree stump, puffed up and intent.

'Come, thou fog-mongering Spirits,' intoned the old sorcerer, whose face looked dirtier than ever. 'Bear me hence.'

He raised his skinny arms, 'Hither, Glabberchops!' he

called. 'To me, Demigorgon! Tarry, Mouldwarp!' But no spirits appeared.

'Disobedient devils! A plague rot thee!' he cursed. 'Wilt thou not come?'

He lifted a strange contraption, made of brooms tied together. They spread out behind him like a sort of bushy fan, as he mounted the foremost and ran round and round the fire.

'Leap through fire to fly away, Salmay, Dalmay, Adonay,' shouted Catweazle jumping over the fire, but instead of flying he collapsed in a little heap, while his train of broomsticks began to burn on the fire behind him.

'Nothing works!' moaned Catweazle.

'Just what d'you think you're trying to do?' said Carrot angrily.

'Thou knot! Thou lump! Thou itch!' snapped Catweazle savagely, mortified at his failure.

'You're a menace, Catweazle, an absolute menace!'

'Pig's grunt!' muttered the magician.

'I knew it was you. It's your fault Sam's in trouble.'

'Scullion! Leave me be!'

'If he goes to jail for something you've done, I'll never forgive you.'

Catweazle ignored him completely and picked up Rapkyn's book, still obsessed with his dream of returning to the past.

'Why do I not fly, Touchwood?' he asked his familiar, giving him a worm to eat.

'You took the brooms, didn't you?' said Carrot. 'Why did you want so many?'

'To jump through the Time Fire,' retorted Catweazle, beginning to climb up to his castle.

'You're potty,' said Carrot, following him up the rusty ladder. 'It won't work.'

'It shall! It must!'

'Not if you used a hundred broomsticks.'

'Canst find an hundred?' asked Catweazle eagerly, pausing at the inspection hole.

Carrot was furious. 'What about Sam?' he said.

'Sam, Sam, Sam,' mimicked Catweazle, going into the tank. 'Sing another song, thou magpie!'

'All right, I'll tell them it was you,' said Carrot bitterly, as he clambered down after him. 'I'll give you away.'

'Nay, thou hast sworn,' said Catweazle, touching Adamcos. 'Thou art my brother.'

'Then you ought to help me,' retorted Carrot.

There was no reply. Catweazle buried himself in Rapkyn's book and reached for a banana.

'No help, no bananas,' said Carrot snatching it from him. 'In fact from now on, no food at all.'

'I will not starve,' said Catweazle brandishing a home-made bow.

'You couldn't hit our barn with that.'

For an answer, Catweazle pointed proudly to a row of rabbit pelts hanging from one of the metal supports. 'My aim is true,' he said conceitedly.

Carrot stared at the bow thoughtfully. An idea was beginning to form in his mind.

'Look, Catweazle –' he began.

'Drip, drip, drip,' said Catweazle peevishly. 'Thou wilt wear me away. I will not help thee. I care nought for thy vassal, thy Sam,' and he turned back to the book.

For a moment Carrot was nonplussed. Then he felt in his pockets. Perhaps a bribe would do the trick. He took out his mouth-organ and began to play. Catweazle, hearing the strange noise, looked round with wonder. Carrot stopped playing and held the mouth-organ towards Catweazle and as the old sorcerer grabbed at it, he moved it out of his range.

'What must I do, brother?' said Catweazle, looking with longing at the mouth-organ.

Carrot squatted down beside him and began to outline his plan.

In the meantime, Sam had arrived at the police station and was rather ostentatiously removing his cycle clips while he chatted to Charlie Cooper, a very young constable he had known most of his life.

'What's this new sergeant like, Charlie?' asked Sam, somewhat nervously.

'You'll find out,' said Charlie, ushering him into Bottle's office.

'Sit down,' said Bottle, without even bothering to look up.

Sam sat down, rather surprised to see his burnt broom on the desk. There was a pause. Bottle looked briefly at Sam and then began writing.

'Mr Woodyard, isn't it?' he said suddenly.

Sam jumped. 'Yes,' he said nervously.

Bottle tapped the broomstick with his pen. 'That yours?' he said.

'Looks like it,' said Sam, puzzled. He decided to make a clean breast of things. 'Do you want to see my licence?'

'That's enough impertinence,' said Bottle tensely. 'Can you identify it?'

'How d'you mean?' said Sam. 'They're all a bit alike, aren't they?'

'In more ways than one,' said Bottle, indicating a row of broomsticks with most of the broom bit burnt off.

'Are you collectin' 'em?' said Sam, beginning to wonder what it was all about.

' 'Ave you ever lit the Beltane Fire?' said Bottle leaning over the desk.

'The which fire?' said Sam, very surprised.

'Ah, then you admit it!' rapped Bottle.

'What?' said Sam, who hadn't admitted anything.

'Lighting the Witch Fire,' said Bottle grimly.

Sam just looked at him blankly.

'Are you or are you not responsible for burning this broom?' said the policeman.

'That's not a crime is it?'

'Not any longer, alas. You are lucky to be living in the twentieth century, Woodyard, and not four or five hundred years ago,' said Bottle pompously. 'Who else is doin' this?'

'Doin' what?' asked Sam, bewildered.

'Holdin' Sabbats in the woods. It's all in here you know,' Bottle continued, showing Sam his copy of *Witchcraft Today*.

'But I don't know anything about witchcraft!' protested Sam, getting very alarmed.

' 'Ow many in the coven?'

'What oven?' asked Sam.

'I shudder to think what abominable practices you people get up to.'

'Listen, Sergeant – '

'I will not have this sort of thing goin' on round Westbourne, interrupted Bottle, wiping his forehead. 'You're stayin' here until I get to the bottom of this.'

But try as he might, Bottle couldn't get Sam to confess to anything. The interrogation had gone on for over two hours when there was a crash of glass and a primitive arrow quivered in the counter where Charlie Cooper sat filling in his Pools.

Sergeant Bottle came out of his office like a charging rhinoceros.

'Great 'Eavens,' he gasped and pulled out the arrow, again carefully using his handkerchief. There was a message wrapped round the arrow and Bottle unfolded it with trembling hands.

> 'Sam is innocent, set him free,
>   In the churchyard, there I'll be,'

he read in an awed voice. 'It's signed Beelzebub, Cooper.

They're comin' out into the open at last,' he breathed.

'Who are, Sergeant?' asked Charlie Cooper.

'You keep an eye on Woodyard,' said Bottle excitedly, as he prepared to leave for the churchyard. 'We've got 'em rattled, my lad. We've got 'em rattled.'

In the churchyard, Carrot and Catweazle crouched behind a pair of ancient headstones.

'I don't think he'll show up,' whispered Carrot.

'He is coming,' said Catweazle tapping his forehead. 'In here are the pictures.'

'But suppose it doesn't work?'

Catweazle took Adamcos from its sheath.

'Thou flap-eared rabbit! I will not fail thee.'

Carrot looked at the knife with some trepidation.

'Don't get carried away,' he said.

'Fear not,' said Catweazle as Bottle appeared in the distance.

'O.K.' said Carrot, crouching down again. 'Give it all you've got!'

Slowly Catweazle rose from behind the gravestone.

Bottle stopped dead when he saw him. 'I have reason

to believe that I have just received a communication from you – on an arrer,' he said, looking at Catweazle with alarm.

' 'Tis so,' said Catweazle warily.

'Er yes, well,' Bottle cleared his throat. 'If you are in any way connected with the disappearances of approximately thirty brooms, I must ask you to accompany me to the station.'

'Thou pudding,' said Catweazle calmly.

'What did you call me?' spluttered Bottle.

'Learn the mysteries,' said Catweazle, beckoning the policeman with a horny forefinger.

'What are you looking at me like that for?' said Bottle, getting a little worried.

Catweazle began to wave Adamcos in front of his face and slowly Bottle's eyes began to glaze over, until he was well and truly in a trance.

'Zazel, Hasmael, Barsabel, Shedbarshemoth. Thou shalt release Sam Woodyard. Set him free,' intoned Catweazle as he hypnotized the policeman. Bottle stood obediently before the sorcerer and then when he was well and truly in a trance, Catweazle turned him round and sent him on his way with a gentle push.

When Bottle returned to the police station, he was breathing heavily and there was a stupid smile on his face. Mr Bennet had arrived, worried by Sam's continued absence, and was arguing with P.C. Cooper. He stopped when Bottle came in, but the sergeant walked straight past them and opened the door to his office.

'You can go, Mr Woodyard,' he said dreamily, 'you can go.'

'Hullo, boss,' said Sam sheepishly as he saw Mr Bennet.

'Case dismissed,' said Bottle in a strange hollow voice. 'Time, gentlemen, please.'

'What?' said Mr Bennet.

'If you want to know the time, ask a policeman,' said Bottle, going into his office and shutting the door.

'The man's ill!' said Mr Bennet.

There was a crashing noise from the office and the sound of running feet. Throwing open the door, the three of them stared at Sergeant Bottle, who was galloping round and round his desk on a broomstick. P.C. Cooper, very embarrassed to see his superior officer behaving in such a manner, pushed them from the door and phoned the Cottage Hospital.

Carrot walked back through the fields with Catweazle and when they reached the wood he silently handed over the mouth-organ. Catweazle's eyes gleamed as he snatched it and darted off among the trees. Carrot listened for a minute and then the rather melancholy sound of the mouth-organ floated back to him.

'Well, I suppose he did earn it,' he said softly to himself.

13

THE FISH OUT OF WATER

CATWEAZLE was worried. It was nine days since the young sorcerer from the farm had been to see him, and now Touchwood was missing as well. He felt very uneasy as he gazed hopefully into his scrying glass, but the Eye of Time was shut and he could see nothing. 'Where art thou, Touchwood?' he muttered anxiously. 'Where hast thou gone?'

He would have been even more worried had he known that Touchwood was squatting in the middle of the farmyard. He tried, too late, to crawl out of the way as Carrot and another boy, both in their school blazers, cycled in through the gate.

Now that Carrot had started school again, Mr Bennet had needed a housekeeper and unfortunately Mrs Skinner was the only applicant. She and her son Arthur had been at Hexwood now for just over a week, and Carrot loathed them both.

'Cor! What a bloomin' great frog,' said Arthur, a spotty boy with glasses.

'It's not a frog – it's a toad,' said Carrot, recognizing Touchwood.

But as he went to pick him up, the other boy pushed him out of the way and ran off into the barn with Touchwood.

'Put him down Arthur,' yelled Carrot, running after him. But Arthur dodged behind the tractor and waved Touchwood at him with a mocking grin.

'Hand him over,' pleaded Carrot.

'Not likely,' said Arthur. 'I saw it first.'

'What d'you want him for?'

'Experiments,' Arthur said evilly.

Carrot gulped. 'Look, Arthur,' he said. 'I'll buy him off you.'

'No dice,' sneered Arthur. 'It ain't for sale. It's my frog.'

'Ten bob,' said Carrot.

' 'Ow much?' said Arthur, very surprised.

'Ten bob,' repeated Carrot firmly.

'You ain't got ten bob. My mum says you Bennets ain't got nothin' 'cept the farm, and that's falling to bits, but you're stuck up just the same,' said Arthur, and waved Touchwood in Carrot's face.

'Don't do that!' said Carrot anxiously.

'Frogs can't feel anything,' said Arthur. 'They're cold blooded.'

'All right,' said Carrot. 'You can have my telescope as well if you give me Touch – if you give me the toad.'

'Done,' said Arthur, absolutely staggered, and handed Touchwood over.

Before he could follow, Carrot ran across the yard and hid Touchwood in the garage. Then he watched as his enemy came out of the barn and went into the house.

'Hullo, Arthur,' said Mr Bennet as the spotty youth came into the kitchen. 'Glad school's over for the week? Where's Carrot?'

'Dunno, Mr Bennet. I told him it was tea-time and that everybody would be waiting,' said Arthur slyly.

'Good boy,' murmured Mrs Skinner.

'I tried to make him come with me, but he just ran off.'

'Oh, did he!' said Mr Bennet angrily.

'Shall I see if I can find him?' said Arthur, but at that moment Carrot came running in.

'Sorry I'm late,' he said while his father gave him a dirty look.

'Where have you put him, Eddie?' asked Arthur.

Carrot, who hated being called Eddie, glared at him. 'That's my business,' he said.

'Put who?' asked Mr Bennet.

'We found a frog,' said Arthur.

'Don't keep calling it a frog,' shouted Carrot angrily, 'it's a toad!'

Arthur lowered his eyes and got quietly on with his tea while Mr Bennet looked at Carrot. 'You'll have to do something about your temper, my lad,' he said.

'I found it really,' Arthur went on maliciously. 'But Eddie's given me his telescope for it.'

'What?' said Mr Bennet.

'Yes,' said Arthur, rubbing it in. 'And ten bob.'

'What? For a toad?' said Mr Bennet. Carrot nodded miserably.

'Whatever for?'

'Just didn't want me to have it, did you Eddie?'

Carrot could contain himself no longer. He leapt to his feet, and grabbed Arthur and the two of them crashed to the floor, rolling over and over. Mr Bennet managed to pull them apart.

'Go to your room,' he ordered Carrot.

Carrot marched out, unrepentant, with a final murderous glance at Arthur.

'Are you all right, dear?' said Mrs Skinner, kneeling over Arthur, who was pretending to be badly hurt.

'Yes, Mum, I think so,' he said bravely.

'I can't have your son bullying my Arthur,' said Mrs Skinner looking up at Mr Bennet. 'He's not strong.'

'He won't, Mrs Skinner,' said Mr Bennet, infuriated by Carrot's behaviour. 'I can promise you that.'

Arthur got unsteadily to his feet. 'I'd better find out why I've upset him,' he said as he left the room.

'He's got such a forgiving nature,' said Mrs Skinner. 'Takes after me of course. We're all very sensitive in my family, you know, especially my brother. Mind you, we don't go to see poor Sid very often now. Was the black pudding all right?'

'What? Oh yes. Fine, fine,' said Mr Bennet still worried about Carrot's outburst.

'I don't think we can stay if there was going to be any more trouble.'

'Don't worry, Mrs Skinner,' said Mr Bennet anxiously, 'Carrot's just got to learn a bit of give and take, that's all.'

Upstairs, Arthur poked his head round Carrot's bedroom door. 'I've come for my telescope,' he said, 'and the ten bob.' Carrot gave them to him without a word.

'What are you going to do with the frog?' asked Arthur inquisitively.

'That's my business,' said Carrot.

'Taking it to your hideout?' asked Arthur casually.

Carrot looked up sharply. 'What d'you mean?' he said.

'In the woods somewhere ain't it?' pressed Arthur.

'I haven't got a hideout,' said Carrot.

'Oh yes you have. Sam said you was always going off somewhere in the holidays.'

'You've got the telescope,' said Carrot. 'Now get out.'

'O.K. mate,' said Arthur going to the door. 'I can take a hint. But I'll find it, you see if I don't.'

Carrot sat for a long time wondering how he could get Touchwood back to his master without Arthur following him. He hadn't dared visit Castle Saburac since the Skinners had come to the farm but now he simply had to risk it. He emptied his satchel, put Touchwood carefully inside, and climbed swiftly down the creeper which grew outside his bedroom window. He ran to his bike and pedalled off up the lane, glancing behind to make sure Arthur wasn't following. He did not know that a thin trail of sugar was beginning to trickle from a small hole in his saddle-bag.

As Carrot went out of sight, Arthur, who had been hiding near the bikes, set off in pursuit, following his cunningly prepared trail.

Carrot, quite unaware that he was being followed, reached Castle Saburac and with a final look round, climbed up to the water tank.

Catweazle sat in his magic circle eating blackberries. His thumbs had been pricking for some minutes, so he was not surprised to see Carrot.

'Thou crawling belly-ache!' said Catweazle reprovingly, as he took the toad in his bony fingers. 'Why did'st thou stray?'

'He was at the farm,' said Carrot, 'You owe me ten bob and a telescope.'

Touchwood croaked almost apologetically and crawled on to Rapkyn's book.

'If he wanders off again,' said Carrot, 'you'd better get him a lead.'

'Where hast thou been?'

'Well school's started again you see,' said Carrot.

'Hast thou brought fire sticks?'

'You never listen,' said Carrot. 'School's started again, and we've got the Skinners.'

' 'Tis a plague?' said Catweazle, drawing back in alarm.

'I'll say! I only wish I could get rid of it.'

'Hast thou no cure?'

'It's *people*, Catweazle.'

'Ah,' said the old man, shaking his head, 'there is no cure for people.'

Carrot explained about Arthur and his mother. 'I'd just like Dad to hear what they say behind his back. He'd soon chuck 'em out. Sam says Mrs Skinner reminds him of a horse his father had. He said they had to shoot it.'

'Evil oft wears a smile. Let us plague them with Demons.' Catweazle pushed Touchwood off the book and began looking for a suitable spell.

'I think the demons would get the worst of it,' said Carrot bitterly. 'I'd better get back. Look after Touchwood.'

'Thou art changed, my brother,' said Catweazle, looking at him intently.

'No, not really,' said Carrot. 'It's just that, well, I can't come to see you so often. The holidays are over now.'

Catweazle sighed. 'Soon I must garner the nuts and prepare for the Long Sleep,' he said.

'You mean you're going to hibernate?' said Carrot.

'I know of no way, no spell to carry me back to mine own time. I choke in this unknown world, a fish out of water,' said Catweazle, who was feeling very sorry for himself.

'Look, I'll try and come tomorrow,' said Carrot.

'Thou wilt bring the curved fruit – the bananas?'

'If I can make it. I'm in trouble with Dad, you see.'

Suddenly, Catweazle's thumbs pricked violently as Arthur began to climb the ladder below. He grabbed

Touchwood and hid under his bed of straw, like a fox going to earth, just as Arthur's head appeared at the inspection hole.

'I said I'd find it didn't I, Eddie?' he grinned.

'If you come in here, Arthur,' warned Carrot, 'I'll give you a thumping you'll never forget.'

'Don't you worry,' jeered Arthur. 'I ain't coming in. I'm going back to the farm to tell your Dad all about it. This is the end of your little hideout, mate,' and he laughed as he began to climb down again.

There was a pause and then Catweazle emerged from the straw, his old joints cracking. The two of them looked apprehensively at each other.

'What are we going to do?' said Carrot.

'Fear not,' said Catweazle grimly. 'Thou and I shall draw his venom.'

'But Catweazle –'

'Go,' ordered Catweazle. 'Remember thy oath. Say nothing of me and on the morrow we will be revenged.'

It was useless to argue, so Carrot went home to the worst dressing down he had ever had from his father, while the Skinners stood by, hardly bothering to conceal their pleasure.

'Not only were you trespassing,' stormed Mr Bennet, 'but you could easily have been killed. That tower is not safe. You're lucky it didn't collapse around you. From now on, as far as you're concerned, those woods are out of bounds.'

The next day, before breakfast, Mr Bennet told Sam all about it while Carrot stood by, red-faced and unhappy.

'There's a reel of barbed-wire somewhere,' said Sam. 'If I wind it all round the ladder an' all, no one'll be able to get up there.'

'Good idea,' said Mr Bennet as he drove the tractor off

to the turkey pens with Arthur sitting triumphantly beside him.

'Thought you'd got more sense,' said Sam. 'All the same, he shouldn't have told on you like that.'

'Do you have to do it now, Sam?' said Carrot desperately, following him into the barn.

'The sooner the better, I reckon,' said Sam, glancing around. 'No it ain't in here,' and he went out leaving Carrot wondering miserably what would happen to Catweazle.

There was a croak behind him. It was Touchwood! Carrot found him behind the bales of straw watching Catweazle, who was kneeling on the ground carefully stirring a milk bottle full of a brackish looking mixture.

'Thank goodness you're here!' said Carrot.

'I am come for our revenge,' said Catweazle, busily stirring away. 'Where is the young snake?'

'He's helping Dad. And his Mum's getting breakfast ready. What's that stuff?' asked Carrot looking at the milk bottle.

' 'Tis the Wisdom of Solomon,' said Catweazle, his eyes glittering mysteriously. 'Give them a drink of this and thy father shall see them as they are. They shall speak from their black hearts.'

'Pongs a bit,' sniffed Carrot. 'Sure it's not poisonous?'

' 'Twill draw out their poison,' said Catweazle, picking up a sack containing his magical belongings. 'Now I shall return to my castle.'

'But you can't!' said Carrot. 'Sam's going to put barbed-wire all over the ladder. It's sort of iron thorns,' he explained hurriedly.

'Men make iron thorns?' said Catweazle.

'That's right. So now you can never go back,' said Carrot.

'Never?' said Catweazle, after a long pause.

'The loft's about the only place. We'll just have to risk it,' said Carrot. But before they could make a move they heard the tractor returning, and Carrot pushed Catweazle behind the bales again. Silently, the magician handed him the milk bottle.

'O.K.' said Carrot rather dubiously, 'I'll give it a go. But keep out of sight and don't move away from here.'

He went out to the tractor and Arthur grinned nastily at him. 'Can I help, Dad?' said Carrot ignoring his enemy completely.

'No,' said his father, 'I'm showing Arthur the ropes. Stop moping about and go and give Mrs Skinner a hand with the breakfast. We won't be long.'

Mrs Skinner sniffed as Carrot came into the scullery. 'Where's Arthur?' she said.

'He's helping Dad,' said Carrot, hiding the milk bottle behind him. 'Shall I lay the table?'

Mrs Skinner nodded so he went through to the kitchen and began to put out the knives and forks. Next he filled three glasses with orange juice, but topped the fourth one up with the magic potion. He was only just in time as his father and Arthur arrived for breakfast.

Mr Bennet poured milk on his cornflakes and then sniffed the jug.

'Something wrong?' asked Mrs Skinner peevishly.

'I'm afraid the milk's turned,' said Mr Bennet, draining his orange juice. Mrs Skinner pursed her thin lips, brought fresh milk from the scullery and then replaced Mr Bennet's cornflakes.

'Er, thank you,' said Mr Bennett, 'but I don't think I want any now, after all.'

Mrs Skinner controlled herself with an effort and to Carrot's horror passed Mr Bennet her glass. 'Have some more?' she said. 'I'm not very keen on the stuff.'

'Thanks,' said Mr Bennet.

'I'll get your bacon and eggs,' she said coldly, going out

175

to the scullery. Mr Bennett raised the glass to his lips and Carrot deliberately knocked over his own.

'You clumsy idiot!' said Mr Bennett, lowering the potion, while Mrs Skinner plonked down his plate and marched out yet again to fetch a dish cloth, an expression of martyrdom on her face.

On her return, she caught Mr Bennet sniffing at the orange juice.

'It's all from the same tin,' she said in an ominously quiet voice and, taking it from him, drank the potion. 'Perfectly all right,' she said.

Mr Bennet looked at his plate again. 'I'm awfully sorry, Mrs Skinner,' he said, 'but I suddenly don't feel very hungry.'

Now whether it was the potion or just her own bad temper Carrot never knew, but Mrs Skinner suddenly went berserk.

'Men!' she screamed, smashing her glass on the floor.

'Mum!' said Arthur, very alarmed.

'You great bully!' shouted Mrs Skinner, pointing a quivering finger at Mr Bennet, who sat looking at her in astonishment. 'Think you're Lord of the Manor, don't you? Ordering people about!'

'Now look here, Mrs Skinner – ' began Mr Bennet.

'She's having one of her turns,' said Arthur.

'You'd 'ave 'im down the mines if you could,' Mrs Skinner went on shrilly, pointing to Arthur. 'Down the mines!'

'What on earth's the matter with you?' said Mr Bennet standing up.

'You can't own us!'

'I don't want to own you!'

'Worn my fingers to the bone I have, working for you!'

'Don't be ridiculous – you've only been here a week.'

'Oh, so now I'm ridiculous, am I?'

'You'd better go and calm down, Mrs Skinner,' said Mr Bennet, moving towards her.

'Keep away from me!' shouted Mrs Skinner, white with fury. 'You lay a finger on me and I'll go straight to the police!'

'You're hysterical!'

'How dare you! It's lucky for you Arthur isn't a bit bigger.'

'What?' said Arthur, worried.

'Don't answer back,' snapped his mother.

'I didn't say anything,' protested Arthur.

'Yes you did! Yes you did!'

'I have had enough,' thundered Mr Bennet.

'You've had enough,' yelled Mrs Skinner. 'I've had more than enough.'

'Then you'd better go,' said Mr Bennet angrily.

'Don't you worry,' shrilled Mrs Skinner. 'We're not staying here another minute. Come along Arthur, we're packing. You wait till my sister in Margate hears about this!' And dragging the protesting Arthur behind her, she slammed out of the room.

Mr Bennet sat down slowly. 'Well, that's that,' he said. 'They didn't last long, did they?'

Carrot was delighted. He left his father still wondering what all the fuss was about and ran back to the barn.

'You did it! You did it!' he told Catweazle gleefully. 'What on earth did you put in that stuff?'

'Bug-bane, barren-wort, penny-cress and blood-root, catchfly, toad-flax, nap-weed and wormwood,' said Catweazle.

'Crumbs!' said Carrot picking up the ladder. 'No wonder it worked!'

The loft door was high up on the end wall of the barn and almost directly over a large water butt. Carrot climbed the ladder and opened the loft door. Behind him

Catweazle heaved up his sackful of belongings, and then over-balanced and toppled into the water butt. A second later, Sam drove past in the farm truck and Carrot pulled the loft door shut and prayed that he wouldn't spot Catweazle floundering in the water.

As the magician surfaced, a strange thing happened. The farm truck melted away before his astonished eyes. The farm buildings shimmered and became transparent, finally disappearing altogether. All around him lay the waters of the lake and beyond stood the giant trees of his forest. Slowly the vision faded and he found himself back in the water butt.

'Did Sam see you?' asked Carrot, opening the loft door.

'Oh! Oh! Oh!' groaned Catweazle, terrified out of his wits.

'Come on!' said Carrot, 'before he comes back.'

Catweazle staggered up the ladder and collapsed in a sodden heap. 'Water,' he gasped. 'All was water!' Carrot wrapped some sacks round him. 'Try and keep warm,' he said. 'You're O.K. now.'

'I was alone,' said Catweazle, his teeth chattering uncontrollably. 'The earth melted.'

'Yes,' said Carrot. 'Well don't worry about it. Everything's fine. We've got rid of the Skinners.' He opened the loft door. 'I'll be back,' he said.

Left alone, Catweazle sat and thought long and hard about the vision he had had in the water butt.

'A fish out of water!' he repeated. 'Out of water!'

And then suddenly everything became clear to him.

'Thou fool, Catweazle,' he said to himself, '*Water* is thy magic. *Water* is thy fate.' He took Touchwood from his pocket. 'Minion,' he smiled, holding the toad against his thin cheek, 'I have found the way back!'

14

THE FINAL MAGIC

SEVERAL days later, as dawn broke over Kingfisher lake, Catweazle threw a stone into the water and watched the circles spreading wider and wider; he knew that, for him, they were magic circles. Only by entering the lake could he return to his own time, and he felt that the pond at the farm just wasn't deep enough. It had taken some time for him to screw up his courage because he was afraid the Normans would be waiting for him. He went back to the loft and began to pack.

It was Mr Bennet's birthday, and rather a gloomy one. Unfortunately he had stuck a fork through his foot a few days before and had been ordered to bed by the doctor. His sister had left her comfortable London flat to look after him but he was a bad patient, and lay restlessly in bed, worrying about the break in the farm routine. Also, he was dreading the ritual birthday tea that his sister was bound to prepare for him.

'I want to get up,' he said, as she bustled in with his lunch.

'Oh dear,' she said, fussing round him. 'You were just like this when you had chicken pox.'

'Now, Flo,' said Mr Bennet, 'you can't possibly remember that!'

'Of course I can,' she said. 'Mother let me stay up and read you *Treasure Island*. It was when I first saw the Hexwood ghost, remember?'

Mr Bennet smiled. His sister had been seeing the Hexwood ghost most of her life.

In the garage, Carrot was watching Sam put the finishing touches to a beautiful metal pipe-rack he had made.

'D'you think he'll like it?' said Sam anxiously.

'I think it's great,' said Carrot.

'What are you giving him?' said Sam.

Carrot proudly took a large car-lamp from a cardboard box. 'This red thing flashes on and off, and it's got a terrific beam,' he explained.

'Smashin'!' said Sam, 'he'll like that. By the way Carrot, you ain't had my welding mask have you?'

'No,' said Carrot.

'It's been missin' a couple of days. An' my bicycle pump an' all.'

'I haven't seen them,' said Carrot, thinking immediately of Catweazle. 'I'll have a look round.'

Still with his present under his arm, he went angrily to the loft, where he found Catweazle sitting with the welding mask on his knees. He looked up guiltily as Carrot came in.

'I've told you before about pinching things,' said Carrot. 'That belongs to Sam.'

' 'Tis to protect me,' snapped Catweazle, 'from the Normans.'

Carrit sighed and took it from him. Then he peered into Catweazle's sack. 'Have you taken anything else?' he asked.

' 'Tis mine, 'tis mine,' said Catweazle, trying to wrest the sack from him, but Carrot fended him off and eventually recovered the bicycle pump.

'Soon I shall be gone,' said Catweazle grabbing the sack.

'That's a good idea,' said Carrot heartlessly. 'Where to?'

'Mine own time,' said Catweazle, eyeing Carrot's cardboard box. 'What hast thou there?'

'You're not having this,' said Carrot. 'It's Dad's birthday present,' but he took the lamp out and showed it off to Catweazle.

'Electrickery!' gasped Catweazle beginning to fizz with fear and excitement. He took the lamp and shone it straight into Carrot's face. Carrot flinched and shielded his eyes from the beam.

''Twould drive away the Normans!' said Catweazle delightedly.

'You aren't having it. It's for Dad.'

'I beg thee –'

'No, Catweazle.'

'I beseech thee –'

'No,' said Carrot, putting it back in the box.

'Not for thy brother?' said Catweazle, switching to a pathetic tone.

'I wish you'd stop calling me your brother,' said Carrot. 'You're too old to be my brother.'

'Come,' said Catweazle, diving into his sack and producing a pair of bedroom slippers. 'I will barter with thee.'

'You've got a nerve!' said Carrot. 'They're mine! I've been looking all over for them. What else have you got in there?'

Catweazle hastily put the bedroom slippers back and clasped the sack to him like a miser with a hoard of gold.

''Tis mine,' he snarled, 'all mine!'

'Hand it over,' said Carrot, getting it from him, 'I'm going to have a good sort through this lot.'

'Thou jackdaw!'

'Look who's talking! You'll get it back. I won't take *your* stuff.'

'Hog-snout!' cursed Catweazle. 'Slug-juice!'

'I keep you out of trouble,' said Carrot. 'Feed you, clothe you –'

'Ant's egg!'

'And look after you. And now you turn round and pinch half my things.'

'Go, before I blast thee!' said Catweazle savagely.

'Right,' said Carrot picking up the sack.

'Thou art a nothing!' said Catweazle putting a hand over his eyes. 'I see thee not!'

'Oh go and jump in the lake!' said Carrot as he left.

Catweazle paused, surprised that Carrot seemed to know his secret.

And then he whispered, 'Ay, thou young fox, I will, when I have thy trickery lantern.'

Aunt Flo was busily piping cream on to a bright green cake when Carrot returned from the loft carrying Catweazle's sack over his shoulder.

'What have you got there, dear?' asked his aunt.

'Er, Dad's present,' said Carrot hastily.

'It's very large,' said Aunt Flo with mild surprise.

'Well, there are other things in here as well,' said Carrot looking goggle-eyed at the cake.

'The icing was meant to be *pale* green,' explained Aunt Flo, 'like your father's aura.'

'His what?' said Carrot.

'His aura, dear. We've all got one you know. Yours is pink. It's a sort of halo, all round you.'

'Have you got one?' asked Carrot.

'Oh yes,' said Aunt Flo. 'Mine's violet.'

'But why can't I see it?' said Carrot.

'You have to be very carefully trained,' said his aunt matter-of-factly.

Carrot took the sack upstairs, dumped it in his bedroom and went in to see his father who was sitting up reading the *Farmer and Stockbreeder*.

'Aunt Flo's made a smashing cake,' grinned Carrot. 'It's bright green. She says it matches your aura.'

Mr Bennet laughed. 'How are you and Sam managing?' he asked.

'Wally's coming to help tomorrow,' said Carrot. 'He might be able to stay till Thursday.'

'Good,' said Mr Bennet, 'I should be up by then if the

doctor knows his stuff.' He nodded towards the chess board by the bed. 'It's your move, by the way,' he said.

While Carrot and his father played chess, Catweazle, now determined to steal the trickery lantern, crept into the scullery and peered round the kitchen door at Aunt Flo still busy with the cake. Silently, he passed behind her and went into the hall. But as he began to mount the stairs, she turned and caught a glimpse of him. She gasped with delight. It was the Hexwood ghost! Never had she seen him more clearly! She looked up the stairs and saw him going into Carrot's bedroom. It had been her bedroom when she was a child and it was where she had first seen the ghost.

She followed, her heart thumping excitedly as she opened the bedroom door. Catweazle spun round and the two of them stared at each other.

'Do try very hard not to disappear,' whispered Aunt Flo to Catweazle, who wished devoutly that he could.

'We're very much in tune, don't you think?' went on Aunt Flo, after a pause.

Catweazle decided to try hypnotism and waved Adamcos at the strange little woman. 'Shedbarshemoth,' he intoned, 'Betharshesim.'

'I can hear you, I can hear you!' cried Aunt Flo, clapping her hands with delight.

'I am invisible,' said Catweazle hopefully.

'No you're not,' said Aunt Flo. 'It's a most beautiful materialization.'

'Invisible,' went on Catweazle, getting worried and waving Adamcos frantically.

'I can't even see through you,' said Aunt Flo. 'You are clever!'

'Nothing works!' moaned Catweazle.

'Oh, don't say that. I'm here to help you.'

'Help?'

'Of course, you poor earthbound thing.'

'I must return,' said Catweazle, realizing Aunt Flo meant him no harm.

'Yes, yes, you must,' said Aunt Flo. 'It must be horrid for you stuck here like this. You've been on the astral plane far too long.'

'I have nowhere,' said Catweazle, enlisting her sympathy.

'I know, and it's terribly bad for you,' she said, coming a step nearer. 'You've always been so shy before. I've seen you several times since I was a girl. And there was that nun one Christmas in the cellar, but I don't suppose you ever bump into her.'

'Where is the boy?' asked Catweazle, who was finding Aunt Flo difficult to follow.

'Do you mean Carrot?'

'Our paths have divided.'

'Has he seen you?'

'Many times.'

'It obviously runs in the family.'

'Thou hast the Power?' asked Catweazle hopefully.

'It comes and goes a bit you know,' said Aunt Flo modestly.

'Miss Bennet?' called Sam from the bottom of the stairs.

'Don't vanish,' said Aunt Flo to Catweazle shutting the door behind her as she went to see what Sam wanted.

'Could I see the boss?' asked Sam coming up the stairs. Aunt Flo smiled at him. 'I've something to show you,' she said.

'What?' said Sam.

'Empty your mind,' she said. 'It may look very shadowy to you,' and she opened Carrot's bedroom door again. Catweazle was hiding under the bed.

'Oh dear, he's gone,' said Aunt Flo, very disappointed.

'Who, Carrot?' said Sam.

'No, the ghost, the Hexwood ghost.'

'Oh. You bin seein' him again, Miss Bennet?' said Sam nervously, as they went down the corridor to Mr Bennet's room.

'I've been talking to the ghost, George,' said Aunt Flo, 'in Carrot's bedroom.'

'What did he look like?' asked her brother, keeping a straight face.

'Oh, you know, a beard and a long robe.'

'I hope you invited him to the birthday tea,' said Mr Bennet solemnly.

'Oh, George, you never take me seriously,' said his sister. 'But I did see him and he says he knows Carrot terribly well,' and, very disappointed that no one would believe her, poor Aunt Flo went downstairs to get things ready. Carrot, very suspicious that Catweazle had something to do with the ghost, left Sam and his father deep in the technical problems of the farm, and went cautiously to his bedroom. He threw open the door and caught Catweazle just as he was trying to dive under the bed again. He hauled him out, determined to get rid of him once and for all.

'I'm fed up with you,' he said. 'First thieving, and now burglary. What do you mean by pretending to be a ghost? I said I'd let you have your stuff back. Couldn't you wait?'

'I will go, I will go,' whined Catweazle.

'All right,' said Carrot. 'Now listen. Wait till we're all downstairs having tea, then creep out through the front door. Find somewhere else to live. The Welsh mountains or the north of Scotland. But keep away from this place, because I've had enough of you,' and Carrot picked up the cardboard box, and left Catweazle staring after him.

The birthday tea was a great success. Aunt Flo had put masses of candles on the cake and after Mr Bennet had blown them out it was time for the presents. Same presented him with the pipe-rack.

'That's really excellent, Sam,' said Mr Bennet. 'It's beautifully made. Thank you very much.'

'Many happy returns, George dear,' said Aunt Flo, who had quite forgiven him about the ghost. Mr Bennet stripped the wrapping from an enormous sweater.

'I hope I made it big enough,' said Aunt Flo.

'I think so, Flo,' smiled Mr Bennet. 'Thank you.'

Then it was Carrot's turn. 'Here Dad,' he said, handing his father the box.

'Gosh, what's this?' said Mr Bennet.

'Something for the farm,' said Carrot. 'You'll never guess.'

'Then let's have a look,' said Mr Bennet.

He opened the box and took out a large crystal ball on an ornamental stand. Everyone, including Carrot, stared at it with amazement. Catweazle had played his final trick. He had taken the lamp and left his scrying glass in its place. Mr Bennet concealed his bewilderment and a broad grin spread over his face.

'Carrot,' he said finally, 'you're a genius.'

'But I – ' began Carrot.

'I think it's terrific.'

'What?' said Carrot amazed.

'It's the most original birthday present I've ever had.'

There was a bang from the front door. 'The rotten old crook!' thought Carrot.

'But I thought – Sam began.

'You know something,' interrupted Mr Bennet. 'Every farmer should have one of these. Thank you Carrot.'

'You mean – you like it?' said Carrot.

Mr Bennet peered into the glass. He had sensed that there was something mysterious about the gift and that Carrot was as surprised as he was, but wisely he decided to ask no questions. After all, there had been many unsolved mysteries that summer. He looked up from the crystal. 'The future looks very bright indeed,' he said smiling at Carrot.

The future looked bright for Catweazle, too, as he prepared for his great journey. The sun was setting over the lake as he muttered his final spells and threw his remaining herbs into the fire. Beside him, on the bank, lay an electric light bulb, a box of matches, a banana, Rapkyn's book, Touchwood's roller skate, the telephone receiver, and the mouth-organ.

'Behold the treasures I have gleaned, Touchwood,' he chuckled, wrapping them in a ragged towel. 'See *my* electrickery,' he said, and switched on the stolen car lamp and waved it at his familiar. Then he placed the bundle on the end of his hazel wand, put the toad in his pocket and lowered himself gingerly into the icy water.

As he waded out up to his waist, Carrot came running up to the lakeside. 'Hey,' he shouted. 'Give me back Dad's present!'

'He hath the scrying glass,' replied Catweazle.

'That's not the point,' said Carrot. 'Give it back.'

'I have need of it. 'Twill protect me from the Normans.'

'You're off your head.'

'They will fear it,' said Catweazle, moving a little deeper.

Carrot stared at him. 'Are you fishing or something?' he asked.

'Nip-bone! I go to my cave in the great forest.'

'Don't be silly. Come on out. You're mad.'

'I am not mad.'

'Yes you are, completely potty. The whole thing's a delusion. Like thinking you're Napoleon.'

'I am Catweazle.'

'You'll get pneumonia.'

'Thou shalt see,' said Catweazle, who was up to his chest in water by now.

'Don't be daft,' said Carrot, getting a little anxious. 'Come on out!'

'Sator, Arepo, Tenet, Opera, Rotas!' chanted Catweazle, waving the car lamp from side to side.

'It can't work, Catweazle,' said Carrot. 'Stop making a fool of yourself.'

'Maggot!' said Catweazle.

'All right then,' said Carrot, folding his arms. 'Go on, disappear!'

Catweazle shut his eyes and concentrated hard. 'Salmay, Dalmay, Adonay!' he cried. But when he opened his eyes, he was bitterly disappointed to find he was still there.

'You'll have to do better than that,' laughed Carrot from the bank.

'O Spirits of the earth, air, fire and thou, O my magic Spirit of water. I call on thee! Sunandum! Hurandos! Salmay! Dalmay! Adonay!'

Catweazle waved the lamp wildly and dropped it in the water. He ducked under and tried vainly to retrieve it before spluttering to the surface again.

Carrot laughed uncontrollably and then stopped suddenly. Something very strange was happening. Catweazle was slowly becoming transparent! Carrot rubbed his eyes in amazement.

'Catweazle!' he called, hardly able to speak with excitement.

'Ay, boy?'

'Something's happening to you. You're – you're – melting!'

'Then 'tis beginning,' replied Catweazle.

'But you can't! Nobody can! I mean, it's impossible!'

'A foolish word,' said Catweazle.

'You're going all misty!'

'Nay, 'tis thou,' said Catweazle. 'Thou art like smoke!'

'But Catweazle – '

Carrot looked at Catweazle. He was a pale shadow above the surface of the lake.

'Then it's true,' he said quietly. 'Everything.'

'Ay, thou doubter! Ay thou disbelieving dreg!'

'Don't go yet,' shouted Carrot suddenly.

'Too late, nettle-face!'

'Please, Catweazle!'

'Nay, Carrot,' smiled the old magician, shaking his head. 'Nine hundred years lie between us. Fare thee well,' and Catweazle turned from the boy and disappeared beneath the water.

'Will you come back one day?' called Carrot.

'One day, one day,' echoed his voice as the mist began to rise, and the magic circles spread outwards over the lake.